NIGHT OF THE BONFIRE

A MICHAEL QUINN NOVEL

KEVIN SCOTT OLSON

SPARTAN PRESS

Reviews for the international bestseller
Michael Quinn novel *Night of the Bonfire*:

"Five stars, worthy of ten... grabs your attention and takes you for a wild ride!" - Goodreads review

"This appealing spy... is ready for his own series." - Kirkus review

"Had me holding my breath and tensing with suspense... can't wait for more." - Amazon review

FOR MORE WORKS BY THE AUTHOR, VISIT
WWW.KEVINSCOTTOLSON.COM

To Sandra, David, Kristin, and Ralene

A portion of the proceeds from the sale of this novel will be donated to the Navy Seals Foundation.

TABLE OF CONTENTS

Laguna Beach, California

IN LLOYD BLACKWELL'S SECRET LIFE, SEVERAL MONTHS OF patient research was about to pay off. The discovery would not just rock the art world—it would rock the *world.*

The tires rolled onto the cobblestones with a familiar bump. Blackwell sighed with contentment as he pulled his black BMW into the driveway of his hillside Laguna home. It had been a good day.

Two hours until he was to meet Marie for dinner. Plenty of time to type up that report and send it in.

He opened the car door and stepped out into the welcoming spring sunshine. The sweet fragrance of jasmine hung in the air as he stopped under the vine-covered portico and punched the keypad buttons to disable the security system. The keypad screen flashed, and the dead-bolts drew back with a resonating click.

There was the slightest sense of movement behind him. Before he could turn, he was shoved against the stucco wall.

Someone twisted his arms behind his back and pressed a gun barrel firmly against the base of his spine.

The jasmine scent was replaced by the pungent smell of a men's cologne.

"Good evening, Mr. Blackwell," a voice spoke in his ear. "We are here to pay you a visit."

"What the hell do you want?" Blackwell's face had been slammed against the stucco with such force that spots swam before his eyes. Blood trickled down from cuts on his face and a split lower lip. He tried to glimpse the men holding him, but a hand on his neck pressed his face against the wall.

"We will discuss everything inside. Cooperate with my men, Mr. Blackwell, or you have drawn your last breath." The voice was calm.

"OK, OK. Take whatever you want. I don't care." The bravado might keep them on the defensive.

The two men holding Blackwell frog-marched him from the portico through the doorway. He blinked to clear away the blood stinging his eyes and stole a glance to each side. The men were bulky and broad-shouldered in cheap suits. Bodyguards for the third man. No chance of overpowering them.

The bodyguards carried him into his foyer as if he were weightless, then stood as they waited for further instructions. Blackwell heard the front door close and lock behind him.

"Hood and cuffs." The voice of the third man came from behind.

A black cloth hood was fitted over his head and tied loosely around his neck with a rope. His wrists were brought around in front and tightly bound by what felt like plastic zip-ties. Next, his ankles were bound with another set of plastic zip-ties.

"The living room sofa."

The two bodyguards obediently dragged Blackwell through the hall, into his living room, and deposited him onto the sofa.

One bodyguard sat on the sofa next to him, gripping his shoulders. There was a scraping noise of wooden chair legs from the chair facing the sofa, then a creak from the wooden seat. The other bodyguard had sat there.

Blinded by the cloth hood, bound hand and foot with his manacled wrists on his lap, Blackwell tried to visualize the scene in his living room, searching for anything that might give him an advantage.

He was sitting near the middle of his sofa. The bodyguard next to him held his shoulders in a pincer-grip. Directly in front of him was the small teak coffee table, and beyond that the wood chair where the other bodyguard now sat facing him. To the right of the sofa was the leather wingback chair, his favorite chair where he liked to sit and read. Beyond the furniture grouping was the picture window to the backyard and, if he could somehow get past both bodyguards and smash through the glass, a chance at escape.

But where was the man who had spoken, the third man?

Footsteps echoed off the travertine tile. The third man walked from the foyer into the living room and stopped somewhere near the coffee table. Then came a metallic clunk of something being set down on the floor, perhaps an aluminum briefcase.

"Quite a charming little home you have here, my friend. A nice art collection, if a bit limited." The disembodied voice spoke as if it were a guest. "Lovely swimming pool. What is this with the pool equipment? Oh yes, this will do."

Footsteps clicked away to the right and stopped. A door opened and closed with a slight squeak—Blackwell recognized it as the side door from the kitchen to the backyard.

He licked the blood off his lips. Nothing could be seen through the fabric of the hood. His senses of smell and hearing were his only source of clues. He smelled the sweat of the bodyguard sitting next to him.

The kitchen door squeaked open and closed again. Clanging noises came from the kitchen, and the footsteps clicked back into the living room. They had the slightly heavy sound of a man's dress shoe.

"Yes, this will do just fine."

Blackwell heard, a couple of feet in front of him, the rustle and plop of falling paper. The man must have swept the art magazines off the coffee table. Next came a soft clank as something metal was placed on the table, followed by the gurgling of liquid being poured into a bowl. An unpleasant chemical odor wafted into the air.

Blackwell's skin began to crawl.

A creak came from the leather wingback chair to the right of the sofa. The third man had sat down there. A sharp metallic click cut through the air.

"Just in case you are harboring any fantasies about escape, Mr. Blackwell, that sound was the slide mechanism of a nine millimeter pistol which is now cocked and pointed directly at your belly." He snapped his fingers.

Another sharp metallic click cut through the air somewhere in front of Blackwell.

"As you have probably surmised, Mr. Blackwell, that second sound was the slide mechanism of another handgun, held by my guard sitting next to me. Its barrel is also trained on your belly."

Blackwell licked the salty blood off his lips and swallowed. The bodyguard sitting next to him gripped him so tightly his arms were going numb. The second bodyguard sat directly across from him with a gun drawn. And the third man sat in the leather wing chair as if he were a guest, a guest with a 9mm aimed and ready.

Even if he could somehow break free from the bodyguard holding him, he would be riddled with bullets before he made it to the picture window.

"The safe is in my bedroom. There's fifty thousand in cash in there, I'll give you the combination. Jewelry's in the top dresser drawer. Take it all and be on your way." It was a desperate gambit, but his best option was to turn this into a robbery.

"Thank you for the kind offer," replied the third man, as if declining a dinner invitation. "We are not interested in your cash or jewelry. We are only after information."

Blackwell stiffened. What could they know? Did they *know*?

"I can put some of your fears to rest, Mr. Blackwell. We have no particular desire to kill you or even harm you. If you provide us with the information we need, we will render you unconscious and then take our leave. We are not in any police database, and we will leave no trace that we were ever here."

The leather sighed as the man leaned back in the wing chair. "I am, among many other things, an art collector like you, Mr. Blackwell. I share your appreciation for the finer things in life. And I am not here after any of your little home collection. Rather, I only desire to know the location of one particular work of art."

"Everything I have is in my gallery."

The man's voice rose in annoyance. "The most valuable artwork in the world? For which so many men have fought and died? No, Mr. Blackwell, we both know it is not hanging in your little gallery."

The leather squeaked softly as the man shifted his position and lowered his voice. "Forgive me. Perhaps you do not fully understand because of what you cannot see. From your backyard, I brought in a white jug of highly concentrated muriatic acid. It is a variation of hydrochloric acid, and it is commonly used to clean swimming pools."

The wing chair creaked, followed by a clank of metal against metal.

"That sound, Mr. Blackwell, was the sound of my gun barrel tapping against a large steel mixing bowl, obtained in your kitchen and now sitting in front of you on your coffee table. That steel bowl is approximately half full of the acid."

For the first time, Blackwell allowed the possibility that this sunny afternoon would be his last. He thought how much he would miss Marie, his beautiful Marie.

The voice took on a professorial tone, as if lecturing a student. "Most people have serious misconceptions about the nature of torture. They think it must be done as they see it in movies, with some exotic device. In reality, everything that is needed to successfully interrogate someone through torture can be found in the common household.

"This is so because, should you reflect on it, you would realize that successful interrogative torture is based, not so much on pain, but rather fear."

The third man cleared his throat and continued. "You probably know that if you spill muriatic acid on yourself, you may suffer a slight first-degree burn. You flush the skin with water, bandage the area, and the burn will heal. That is the end of it. If you should be so unfortunate as to spill a larger amount on your bare skin, you may perhaps suffer damage down to the second layer of skin, incurring a second-degree burn, and thus a trip to the local urgent care clinic would be in order.

"However, have you ever considered the effects if your skin —let's say, your hand—was deliberately immersed in the acid and held there?" The voice paused. "In a very short time, the acid will burn through all three layers of skin. Such a third-degree burn will cause massive damage as the acid continues to eat through to the tissue and bone underneath.

"You would, of course, feel great pain. Indescribable pain.

But worse than the pain is the knowledge that you are being horribly scarred and disfigured—forever—as such damage would be far beyond the ability of any plastic surgeon to repair.

"It is such fear, Mr. Blackwell, and not the associated pain, that truly makes for a successful interrogative torture. Pain is temporal; it passes. Many brave soldiers have been conditioned to withstand astonishing amounts. Fear, on the other hand, is quite different.

"Fear, you see, can be *infinite.*"

The cold-blooded words, spoken with clinical detachment, were repulsive. A wave of nausea swept over Blackwell. Inside the hood, the foul air was suffocating.

The voice continued. "It is fear that can make the most strong-willed subject eager to confess every secret he may possess. In your case, my friend it is the fear dawning upon you right now, that you will spend the rest of your life hideously disfigured.

"If you cooperate, you will wake up tomorrow looking very much like you do now. You seem successful and quite fit for an older man. Surely you have a keen interest in your own self-preservation, eh?"

Blackwell's mind raced as he sat silently on the edge of the sofa. There wasn't much time.

"Assuming you are right-handed, we will start with, say, three fingers of your left hand. We may even let you choose which fingers. Then, if necessary, we will proceed to more vital parts of the body. Eventually, we will come to your face. Alas, when we reach that point you will not see for much longer, as we will start first with your eyes."

A scraping noise cut through the air, as the wing chair moved somewhere on the tile.

"From the photographs on your mantel, Mr. Blackwell, it appears you have a girlfriend. And what a lovely young woman she is. You have good taste. She looks like quite the sensual type. I would guess you are passionate about keeping her."

The wing chair scraped again as it dragged across the travertine. A whiff of cologne penetrated the cloth fabric of the hood. The man had moved his chair close. "Perhaps in this case, after your fingers are gone, we should proceed next to your manhood. How long will your pretty girlfriend stay with you after that, Mr. Blackwell, when you are not only blinded and disfigured, but no longer even a man?"

With a sigh, Blackwell sat back on the couch. His shoulders sagged, and his body seemed to go limp. His words came weakly through the cloth hood, and his tone went from defiance to surrender "OK. You win. I'll tell you whatever you want to know. But I'm going to pass out from my circulation being cut off. Can you get your man here to ease up with his grip? I'm not going anywhere."

"Of course," The man snapped his fingers, and the wing chair creaked as he leaned back.

The bodyguard holding Blackwell grunted and slightly relaxed his grip.

Blackwell's hooded head sagged down on his chest in relief. His shoulders slumped, and his feet slid forward slightly until they were resting on the base of the teak table. His handcuffed wrists lay in his lap. He took a deep breath and exhaled.

Three, two, one.

He kicked both feet up at the underside of the small coffee table. There was a *thump* as the table flew up in the air, followed by a *clank* as the steel bowl was launched off the table.

Blackwell jack-knifed his upper torso onto his lap and wrenched off the hood. As he did so, he heard a soft splashing sound and muffled *phffts* as a 9mm bullet, then another, bored into the sofa where he had been sitting.

An excruciating scream came from the man in the wood

chair sitting across from Blackwell, followed by the clamor of a steel bowl and a gun clattering to the tile floor.

The bowl of acid had hit its target.

Blinking to adjust to the light, Blackwell glanced around the room. The bodyguard sitting across from him clawed helplessly at his face, howling in pain. The man's gun lay on the floor near the overturned bowl. The bodyguard sitting on the sofa next to Blackwell leaned forward, caught off guard and clumsily reaching for a gun that seemed to be stuck in a shoulder holster inside his suit coat.

Blackwell lashed out with his right elbow and jabbed the bodyguard's left eye. The man screamed and doubled over. Blackwell wrapped his right arm around the bodyguard's thick neck and shoved the man off the sofa and across the floor onto the flailing body of the other bodyguard. With a loud crash, the wood chair fell over backwards and both bodyguards tumbled to the floor.

His eyes turned to the leather wing chair. There sat the third man.

Blackwell caught a glimpse of a well-dressed man with dark features twisted in a scowl. Then he noticed the man's suppressor-equipped gun barrel moving to take aim, and he immediately dove face-forward onto the floor.

As his face hit the cold tile, there was a *phfft* from the man's gun, and then a sharp burning sensation down his back and a loud *crack* as the bullet ricocheted off the travertine next to him. He lifted his head and saw the sneering face and the 9mm barrel lowering to fire again.

Blackwell sprang up to his right, his manacled hands outstretched and closing in on the moving gun barrel.

CHAPTER 1

Foxfield Ranch, Virginia

THE VIEW FROM THE PICTURE WINDOW behind the Director's desk was, as always, resplendent. A panorama of rolling hills, forested with pine and spruce trees, stretched as far as the eye could see. Late afternoon was passing its torch to early evening, and, while the sky above still held its azure, the rays of the setting sun covered the forest with a golden bronze that darkened to shadow at the corners.

It was the sort of view, thought Quinn, which would bring solace to one who dealt with humans and their quarrels. He had visited Foxfield Ranch and sat in this same red leather guest chair in all seasons, yet every time he walked into the Director's office this view brought a moment of reflection. No doubt the Director himself came here to his private ranch as often as possible, just to escape the incalculable pressures of Langley.

And, of course, the ranch was the designated meeting place for all dealings that were 'off the books.'

The text had come while Quinn was in a bar at the Miami airport, killing time as he waited for his connecting flight home.

His cellphone had beeped with the distinctive tone of a text from Headquarters.

Your flight to California has been cancelled. You are booked on the 9:30 a.m. flight to Dulles. You will be met at the airport and driven to Foxfield. Meeting with Director later in the day, time TBD.

What now? His thoughts wandered as he gazed out the window.

"Good afternoon, Michael. I see you still enjoy the scenery."

The Director strode through the doorway into the large, mahogany-paneled office. He looked the same, agelessly middle-aged. He was dressed, as always, in his navy suit with the faint pinstripes, white shirt, and red military-stripe tie. He walked across the room to his Georgian desk and laid down the battered leather briefcase that always seemed out of place in comparison to the rest of the office. After giving Quinn an appraising once-over, the Director extended his hand.

"Afternoon, sir." Quinn stood and shook hands.

"You're looking well."

"Thank you, sir."

They sat down.

The Director opened his briefcase. He despised small talk and preferred to get right to business. He removed a manila file and leafed through it. "Good work on that Caribbean business."

"Thank you, sir." "Good work" was among the highest compliments one could be paid by the Director.

"Special Operations Command wanted to issue a commendation for your service to your country. As usual, I declined on your behalf."

"Of course, sir."

"They also extended—again—an invitation to join full time, in an official capacity. I assume you would prefer to maintain your current status as an independent contractor?" It was more of a statement than a question.

"I would." The anonymity and privacy of Quinn's life meant too much for him to ever change.

The Director finished leafing through the manila file and put it back into the briefcase. He removed another manila file from which he extracted an eight-by-ten color photograph. He slid the photograph across the desk.

"Recognize him?"

"No sir." Quinn gazed at a man in his mid-to-late fifties, wearing casual khaki clothes.

"Lloyd Blackwell. Joined the CIA about the same time I did. For the past seven years, he's been running an art gallery in Laguna Beach."

"Did he stay with the CIA?"

"Very much so. The art gallery has served as his cover. Do you follow the art world, Quinn?"

"Not at all."

"Neither do I. The take-away, for our interest, is that valuable works of art—paintings, sculptures—have become a major vehicle for the laundering of large amounts of illegitimate funds. Not only for organized crime, but for many of the more sordid regimes we deal with around the world."

"I see."

"Even before he joined the Company, Blackwell was a collector. When he was transferred to California, he got involved with the local art scene there and opened his gallery. It provided an excellent cover. In recent months, he worked himself deep into the black-market underground. Had his finger on something big.

"Vast amounts of drug money were being moved around to purchase one highly valuable work of art. Some sort of legendary painting. A fence, a Russian named Kerensky, had just sold it to the highest bidder. Blackwell alerted us that he was about to file a report with critical information."

"Was?" Quinn sensed a change in tone.

The Director sat up straight and pulled a second photograph from the file. His face darkened as he glanced at it, then he slid it across the desk. "This is what was left of him. His girlfriend found him at his home. She went there when he didn't show up for a dinner date."

Quinn's expression hardened as he gazed at the gruesome photograph. What had been a handsome, athletic man was now unrecognizable. After a minute he placed the picture back on the desk and looked at his superior.

"Acid?"

The Director nodded. "Muriatic acid, the kind used to clean pools. He was tortured with it in the living room of his own home in Laguna Beach. The local coroner has determined that he was also shot several times with a 9mm.

"Blackwell didn't die without putting up a fight. His living room is a hell of a mess. Acid burns in several places, pieces of smashed furniture. He damn well did some damage to his attackers."

The Director removed a flash drive from the file and slid it across the desk.

"Your assignment is to find out what Blackwell was working on and to follow it through. As you'll see from the flash drive, we've added to your resume. You have now been a principal in Global Art Funding LLC for the past five years. They're a real company, with headquarters in New York and offices in Newport Beach, London, and Paris. In your side business as an art dealer with them, you've done rather well."

Quinn picked up the flash drive. This would be a hell of a learning curve. "Sir, I—"

"I know, I know." The Director raised his hand. "You'll be given a crash course in art appreciation. The details are all on the flash drive. Will, your field supervisor, will be in contact.

"And we have intel on this legendary painting, courtesy of an old friend. An Englishman, a professor of art history at Cambridge University who has helped us in the past. He's an expert on such things, and agreed to fly out and meet us." The Director pressed a button on his intercom. "Julia, please send in Professor Hale."

The mahogany door opened, and a pony-tailed young woman ushered in a white-haired man carrying a slim leather briefcase.

The Director stood and made introductions. When he shook hands, Quinn noted the man's firm, dry handshake. The professor sat down in the guest chair next to Quinn.

During the perfunctory small talk, Quinn appraised the visitor. Professor Robert Hale looked to be in his late sixties, of average height, and with the thin build of a runner. He had a ruddy complexion, and his light blue eyes radiated intelligence. His brown sport coat was well-worn, and the gray and white argyle necktie hung in two pieces, as if it was always so. Quinn liked the man instinctively.

The professor produced a tablet computer from his briefcase and placed it on the desk.

"Mr. Quinn, your superior and I go back quite a few semesters. A phone call from him is bound to be interesting. From what I understand, you are now on the trail of what might be one of the most remarkable artworks of all time. Presuming you are, then you are also smack in the middle of a blood feud between two families—one Russian, the other Italian."

"What are they fighting about?"

"The ownership of this particular work of art. A painting that, if it exists, would be one of the most valuable artworks in the world."

"What's so special about this painting?"

"It is the portrait of a lady, and it has a profound effect on viewers. You've heard of the Mona Lisa and her mysterious smile? Something like that. With this portrait, the woman is apparently so, ah, attractive that viewers don't want to take their eyes off of her."

"I see." Quinn glanced at the Director. What kind of odd case was this? "I wish I would have known her."

"As did many." Professor Hale smiled. "Once you see the painting, the legend goes, you have to have it. With some viewers the reaction was delayed, with others it was immediate. Sounds far-fetched, I know, but viewers have been entranced by Mona Lisa's gaze for centuries. I daresay we've all seen women so attractive we didn't want to pull our eyes away."

"One or two," replied Quinn. "Do we know what happened to this painting?"

"It is said to have been destroyed in the Bonfire of the Vanities."

"The Bonfire of the what?"

"I think a brief explanation is in order." The professor sat back in his chair. "This painting was created in Renaissance Italy, during a time when society had moved on from the austerity of the Middle Ages and re-discovered the sensual pleasures of life. Wine, food, sex—after abstaining from these pleasures for so long, the Italians were now enjoying them all. By personifying the allure of female beauty to men, this portrait was, for a short time, the talk of Europe."

"For a short time? Who spoiled the party?"

"For every cycle in history, there is a counter-cycle. Soon there arose an opposition movement that didn't like all this newfound pleasure. Saw it as the end of civilization.

"The movement came to power and began holding public bonfires, calling them the Bonfire of the Vanities. At these bonfires, surrounded by screaming crowds, the citizenry—

often the young and lovely ladies of society—would gather around and throw into the fire anything deemed pleasurable: jewelry, clothing, even works of art."

The professor tapped the tablet screen, and a black-and-white drawing appeared. A crowd, dressed in medieval garb, surrounded a stone fire pit. Flames swirled high as a young woman, her dress torn asunder, cast the piece of fabric into the fire.

"Can you imagine the spectacle?" The professor looked at the screen. "Beautiful women gathered around, screaming and tossing their finest things into the bonfires, surrounded by a torch-bearing mob."

Quinn found the image of the bonfire captivating. "Why would this artist destroy his own work?'

"The artist was now an enemy of the state. Fearful for his life, he threw every one of his works into the Bonfire of the Vanities." The professor paused. "Our story would end there, except, down through the centuries, rumors have persisted that the artist couldn't bear to destroy his greatest work and thus hid his masterpiece from the Bonfire."

"Is there any evidence of its existence?"

"No. No photographs, not even a drawing. There are some general descriptions, and I believe they have been included in the material your superior has provided you. By all accounts, you will know this painting when you see it. And I do hope you find this painting, Mr. Quinn. It would be one of the great treasures of the Western world."

The professor paused. The wrinkles in his face were those of an old man, but the enthusiasm in his eyes was that of a young man. "One last thing. Bit of a long shot, but I did some research on the plane flight over. Those feuding Russian and Italian families each have a living descendant who is an art collector."

The professor tapped the screen again.

"Both descendants are wealthy men in their early forties. They are said to have extensive collections, but operate on the shady side. Afraid I don't know much else about them. Here we are."

Two color photographs appeared on the screen. On the left was a photo of a tanned, dark-haired man in a tuxedo, posing in front of a Mediterranean-style mansion. On the right was a photo of a well-dressed, aristocratic-looking man with angular features and cold gray eyes.

"The impeccably dressed man on the right," remarked the professor, "is the Russian. His name is Viktor Orlov."

The room was silent as the men scrutinized the photographs.

"And the rather arrogant-looking man in the tuxedo, on the left," finished the professor drily, "is the Italian. His name is Marco Leone."

"Don't recognize either man." Quinn looked at the Director. "I suppose it's time I paid them a visit."

The Director had been sitting back, listening. He leaned forward. "This Mr. Orlov lives in Moscow, Michael. A bit of a trek." He pointed at the other picture. "Mr. Leone, on the other hand, lives right near you, in southern California. Moved there from his native Italy three years ago, after making his fortune in pharmaceuticals. Lives large, apparently, as a playboy and art collector. He'll be attending a black-tie charity fundraiser in Laguna Beach this Saturday night.

"And so will you. We've made arrangements for you to meet him there."

CHAPTER 2

Saint Petersburg, Russia

"Do you know who I am?"

The old man nodded. He would have spoken, but the gag in his mouth prevented him from doing so.

"Then you know why I am here."

Viktor Orlov walked in a slow circle around the man, who was standing in the center of the living room of the drab two-bedroom apartment. The two men were polar opposites. The gagged and handcuffed old man was disheveled and dressed in a stained white T-shirt and wrinkled pants. Beads of sweat glistened on his bald pate and rosacea-pink cheeks. His flabby white belly protruded from his T-shirt and hung over his belt.

Viktor Orlov was immaculately dressed. His vicuña overcoat, like his gray pinstriped Huntsman suit and John Lobb loafers, came from Savile Row. The clothes fit loosely on his lean frame. The brown hair was cut short. His facial features were angular, with narrow cheekbones and piercing gray eyes. His bearing was aristocratic, his demeanor imperial.

He held the old man's business card and read aloud from it. "Boris Kerensky. Dealer in Art and Antiquities."

He sighed and put the card back in his pocket. "So. A low-rent pawnbroker tries to make a killing smuggling art." Orlov paused, then spoke as if pronouncing judgment. "*Gospodin* Kerensky, you have committed two great crimes. And both crimes are unforgivable. You have betrayed your country, and you have betrayed me. While the former crime is arguably more serious, it is the latter crime for which you will have immediate consequences."

The old man whimpered through the cloth gag. He glanced at Orlov's two guards, standing on either side of him with their Makarov pistols aimed at his head.

Orlov walked over to the window and looked down eight stories to the narrow street where his black Bentley waited, purring, its white exhaust wafting upward in the cool morning air. A black SUV was parked behind the Bentley. Two men, his driver and another guard, stood between the cars, scanning the area, looking up at the apartment window. Orlov gazed out the window as he spoke.

"You may know *of* me, Kerensky, but apparently you don't know *about* me. My family, we have been movers and shakers in the art world for generations. For decades we have hoped that this work survived. We assumed the worst, that it was destroyed, and prayed for the best, that it might still be somewhere in Russia. And to think it was so close …"

He turned away from the window and walked back to the old man. His voice rose, almost to a shout.

"Did you think we would not discover your treachery? Did you think we were some low-level *Mafiya*? I am one of the new Russians, Kerensky, a man of the world. I have houses in Switzerland and France and a yacht anchored in the Mediterranean. I have business interests all over the globe.

"How do you think I have survived when a Khodorkovsky spends years in Siberia, and a Berezovsky dies alone in exile? My armed men are with me 24/7. Many of them are ex-FSB. Our tentacles reach deep into all levels of the State.

"Did you not think, Kerensky, that a mere pawnbroker such as yourself would be child's play for us to find?"

Orlov paced in a circle around the man. He looked around the humble apartment, at the modest furniture and at the framed photographs hanging on the wall.

He stopped. "You already know you have forfeited your life."

The old man nodded his head.

"That does not mean I am without compassion. All my life I have searched for this treasure. You possess information which may lead me to her.

"If you cooperate, we will let your wife and family live. Your wife will come home today to find you have committed an honorable death by suicide. Your family will grieve, but they will survive and move on and live their lives.

"If you do not cooperate, your death will be spread over three days, and will be of an agony you cannot begin to imagine. And then, Kerensky, my men will do the same to your wife and your children and grandchildren."

The old man was silent, but his eyes blazed with heightened intensity, an involuntary physical reaction as the fear for his own safety was transformed into terror at the thought of what could happen to his family.

"Do you wish to cooperate?"

The old man nodded his head.

"That is wise. *Uberite klyap.*"

One of the guards removed the gag. The man coughed and licked his lips.

"Kerensky, where is the painting?"

The old man swallowed and spoke in a whispered croak.

"Someplace in Italy. I don't know where. Perhaps Rome. There is a large art auction that will be held there."

Orlov took a step closer. "And who was the buyer?"

"An Italian. A man named Leone."

Orlov's eyes narrowed. "You have no idea of the irony involved, Kerensky. But I believe you. Anything else?"

"There was an American spy prying into our affairs. A man named Blackwell. But I have heard he is now dead."

"Good. Did you see the painting?"

"Yes." For a moment the terror vanished from his eyes, and he spoke like a sentimental man recalling a favorite girlfriend. "Yes."

Orlov turned around, looking up at the dingy apartment ceiling. His gaze fell upon an iron bracket attached to the ceiling over the humble dining table. The bracket looked old but sturdy, and had probably once held a chandelier. Standing on one of the dining chairs, Orlov tested the bracket with his body weight.

"This will do." Orlov strode into the master bedroom, then emerged holding a tie in his gloved hands. He nodded at the two guards. "You, move the dining table and chairs over, but leave this one chair under the bracket. You, prepare the noose and tie it to the bracket. Kerensky, stand on the chair when the noose is ready."

Everyone did as they were told. Kerensky stood on the chair while the guard tightened the noose around his neck.

Victor Orlov looked at his watch, then at his guards. "I am finished here. There is much to be done. You two stay here until you are sure he is dead, then remove his handcuffs. Lay the chair on its side so it appears he kicked it away. Make sure the apartment is clean. The SUV will wait for you."

Orlov looked around at the shabby apartment, then strode to the door.

As his hand touched the doorknob, he turned back for a last look. The two executioners were standing on either side of the wooden chair. The condemned man was standing on the makeshift gallows, his eyes on the photographs of his family hanging on the opposite wall.

"*Do svidaniya*, Kerensky." Orlov gave the nod to proceed, then turned and walked away, closing the door behind him.

In the dingy hallway outside the apartment, the scraping sound of the wooden chair penetrated through the thin walls, as did the muffled gurgling that followed.

CHAPTER 3

Laguna Beach, California

His nerves stirring, Quinn turned off Pacific Coast Highway and onto the curving driveway of one of the most beautiful resorts in the world.

Nestled on a bluff overlooking the ocean, the Montage Laguna Beach was a small but luxurious resort that combined a California getaway with old-world charm. For Quinn, the place held pleasant memories, and as he pulled his car up under the portico, the memories bubbled up to the surface.

He handed his keys to the college-kid valet, put the memories away where they belonged, put on his tuxedo coat, and strode through the entryway.

The lobby was a noisy bustle of greetings between guests excited about the evening ahead. The women wore bare-shouldered evening gowns, the men wore the timeless uniform of the black tuxedo. To the left was a woman posing for photographs, with a half-dozen paparazzi fawning around her.

Quinn recognized her as an actress in a string of romantic comedies. What was her name?

To the right was a long, rectangular table covered by a white tablecloth and boxes of envelopes. Above the table, a banner on the wall proclaimed, "Orange County Arts Society Casino Night," and in smaller type below, "Registration Here." He walked over to the table and stood in the line in front of a white card labeled "O–R."

When he reached the table, the blonde girl smiled as she sorted through a box of envelopes.

"Quinn, Michael, where are you, where are you? Ah, here you are. Oh!" She looked up. "I see you're a member of the President's Circle, Michael—er, Mr. Quinn. There's a special reception area for your group, to the right when you enter the casino." As she handed him a plastic name badge and a program for the evening, her hand lingered in his.

As he entered the grand ballroom, Quinn thought for a moment that he had walked into the original Monte Carlo casino in Monaco. The great room had been transformed into a replica of a European casino, complete with gaming tables of carved mahogany and enormous oil paintings on the walls.

In the middle of the room were two large roulette tables manned by tuxedoed croupiers. At the far end, cordoned off with gold stanchions and thick, red-velvet rope, was a *Salon Privée* for the high rollers. The rest of the room contained table after table of lively games of blackjack, craps, and poker.

Throughout the ballroom, nubile cocktail waitresses circulated, their drink trays held high. They were dressed in mock-tuxedos consisting of a black bow tie around the neck and a bare-shouldered, black satin one-piece with the bosom cut so low as to distract the most sedate male gambler.

Quinn ordered a Glenfiddich on the rocks. As the first sip of whiskey began its slow burn down his throat, a hand touched his arm.

"Mr. Quinn? Mr. Michael Quinn of Global Art Funding?"

A matronly, handsome woman stood next to him. She smiled and extended her hand. "Dorothy Bainbridge. I'm chair of the President's Circle. So very nice to meet you. I hope you haven't been here too long. I wanted to greet you personally and welcome you as a new member."

"My pleasure, Mrs. Bainbridge. Quite the evening you have here." Quinn smiled back into pleasing blue eyes. The woman looked to be in her late fifties and wore her years well. The lines in her face had a refreshing honesty. Her bearing projected the good will and peace of one who has lived a full life.

"Please, call me Dorothy. May I introduce you to the other members of the Circle who are here tonight? It's the least we can do for someone who has been so generously supportive of our efforts." Her arm was already in his as she guided him toward the thick velvet ropes that guarded the *Salon Privée*.

The rumble of the casino faded into the background. Behind the velvet ropes of the *Salon* stood a lone table of *Chemin de Fer*, empty save for the croupier. Next to the table, a small group conversed. A cocktail waitress was taking their drink orders.

Dorothy kept her arm in Quinn's as they approached the group. "Everyone, I'd like to introduce you to our newest member, and very generous patron, Mr. Michael Quinn of Global Art Funding."

Two chatting couples turned to greet him. Quinn was introduced to a sixtyish, cerebral-looking man, and his frail-looking wife. Next came a fiftyish, outgoing man and his slender, forty-something wife.

Dorothy's arm stiffened in his arm as she turned to face another group. Out of the corner of his eye, he noticed that her smile now seemed forced.

"And over here we have Mr. Marco Leone of The Leone Company, and his ... friends. Mr. Leone, I'd like you to meet our newest patron, Mr. Quinn."

A dark-haired man, standing with his back to them, chatted with a group of four young women. He turned around, and a tanned, haughty-looking face with raised dark eyebrows and a Roman nose looked Quinn over. There was a whiff of expensive cologne.

"So honored to make your acquaintance, Mr. Quinn." The baritone was authoritative as the man extended his hand.

Quinn prepared himself for the iron grip. *Jackpot.* Marco Basilio Casimiro Leone was his quarry for the evening.

And, he reminded himself, this was a man with absolutely no criminal history. Not even a parking ticket.

"It was my pleasure to have done business with Global Art a couple of years ago." Marco looked at Quinn as if he was appraising him. "A representative from Global Art—a Mr. D'Ambrosio, his name was—helped me obtain an exquisite Delacroix that a private collector had resisted selling for decades. Tell me, is Mr. D'Ambrosio still with your firm?"

"Yes, but he transferred to the London office several months ago. Just before I came to the Newport Beach office."

"I see. Well, we must talk then. Your firm was a valuable resource. Where is that waitress? I didn't get to order my drink. Here, walk with me."

Marco strode a few steps beyond the velvet ropes of the *Salon.* Quinn walked with him. When Marco saw the cocktail waitress, he stopped, held his hands above his head, and then clapped them twice, so loudly that several heads turned in their direction. Marco crooked his finger at the waitress and waited with an impatient look on his face as she made her way over. He ordered a *bicicletta,* specifying equal parts Campari and Pinot Grigio.

After the waitress left, Marco turned his attention back to Quinn. Their conversation continued, the probing dialogue made by two businessmen discreetly sizing each other up. With his outward persona engrossed in the art world, Quinn examined the man's physical features.

Marco stood about six feet tall and looked powerfully built. The lips were thin and stern, in the permanent frown of someone who is always dissatisfied. The Roman nose had a pronounced dorsal hump. Beneath the heavy brow, deep-set dark eyes regarded everything with a probing intelligence. The cold-blooded eyes, combined with the prominent nose, reminded Quinn vaguely of a shark.

The drink came. Marco motioned for Quinn to follow, and strode back toward the *Salon*.

"Your knowledge is impressive. I would like to discuss things further. You are free for lunch tomorrow?"

"Yes, I believe so."

"Great. My place at noon then. You have heard of my Palazzo?"

As they walked back, and as Quinn's first impressions were stored away in his memory banks, he began the process of fine-tuning the details. The thickly heeled dress boots meant that Marco was really about five foot nine. This was a giveaway of a man who was vain enough to wear shoes with a lift. The hair was so jet-black for a man in his mid-forties that it was dyed. The notion of vanity was further reinforced by the monogrammed cuffs protruding from the Brioni tuxedo, and by the manicured, clear-polished fingernails.

The vanity, the arrogance—it all blended together to paint a picture of a narcissist.

But of course, while that might foretell an obnoxious character, it gave no hint of criminality.

They had reached their group behind the velvet ropes.

Marco walked up to his four women. "Ah, you must forgive me." His loud baritone overrode the other conversations.

"My love of art has forsaken my manners." He smiled and gestured at the women. "I must introduce my acquaintances. Mr. Quinn, please meet my friends Jacqueline, Kimberly, and Robin."

Oddly, only three of the four women standing around Marco had been introduced. Voluptuous, raven-haired, and in their late twenties, they had rather hard-looking faces made up with mascara and eyeliner. All three wore what looked like variations of the same standard-issue cocktail dress with varying degrees of suntanned cleavage.

Marco cleared his throat and turned to the fourth woman, who was standing apart from the others.

"And this—" he paused with pride "—is Sienna."

Quinn looked into the most stunning green eyes he had ever seen. His mind searched for a way to record such an unforgettable image. Yes, that was it. He was looking into someone's private emerald sea. A sea whose depths he wanted to explore.

Sienna didn't look anything like the other three. She was younger, in her early twenties, and taller, perhaps five foot seven. Her skin was a smooth, lightly tanned *cafe au lait,* and it looked genuine, without a trace of bronzer. Dark brown eyebrows were set high, framing the eyes. Her full lips looked as if they had a natural pout. The ash-blonde hair was pinned back at the sides, with cascading tresses that fell over her bare shoulders.

She wore a simple but elegant, white evening gown that clung to her athletic figure. The only jewelry was a pearl necklace and a pearl bracelet.

"Nice to meet you, Mr. Quinn." She offered her hand.

"Nice to meet you, Sienna." Realizing he had been staring, he grasped her hand.

There was a moment of awkward silence. Quinn was trying to think of what to say next when Sienna withdrew her hand and looked away.

She had been forced to do so as a shoulder moved in front of her—the broad shoulder of Marco stepping in between them. Marco grasped Sienna's now-free hand with his left hand and put his right hand on Quinn's shoulder. The deep-set eyes stared as he smiled at Quinn.

"You must excuse us. Off we go to the tables. I promised to teach my lovely Sienna the fine art of throwing the dice. We'll see you tomorrow then, at my place. Yes?"

"Looking forward to it." Quinn had been forced to take a step backward.

"Splendid." As the word came out, Marco was already walking away, his hand holding Sienna's, the three other women following behind his bulky shoulders.

Quinn lingered for a while in the *Salon,* chatting with Dorothy and the other couples of the President's Circle. Then, holding up his empty whiskey glass as justification, he excused himself from the group and made his way across the crowded room to the mahogany bar.

When his drink came, he swirled the ice cubes. Mission accomplished, at least for this evening. His finger tapped his whiskey glass as he pondered tomorrow's meeting. A dead end, or was he onto something? Was this blood feud about some artwork for real?

And this lovely girl, this Sienna?

Marco's trophy. Dangerous eye candy. *Pass on her, and concentrate on your mission.*

A glance at his watch told him it was only nine fifteen. Too early to leave. He needed to occupy himself until eleven or so.

Drink in hand, he killed some time at the tables. The players were pleasant, but making the frivolous bets people make when the chips are play money. With no purpose or skill to the games, the noisy chatter grew tiresome.

It was time for a break. Leaving his chips and name badge on a blackjack table, Quinn walked out of the casino and stopped in the men's room. At the black granite counter, he splashed his face with cold water and looked in the mirror.

The man in the mirror, attired in the black tuxedo, was to all appearances the sort of prosperous, thirty-something businessman one might see at the fundraiser. The tousled, medium-brown hair was parted on the side in a business-casual style. The lean jawline was clean-shaven, and the blue-gray eyes appeared calm.

A careful observer of the man in the mirror might have noticed the cold focus of the eyes. The observer might have wondered about the faded, inch-long scar next to the right ear, the scar that had come from an ice pick attack.

Down the hall, through the double doors, and outside to the beach area. The noise of the casino faded away. A walk along the beach would kill some more time.

Clumps of fog drifted in from offshore. The weather had turned cool, and only a few stragglers lingered on the long, curving walkway that bordered the beach. As Quinn stopped to warm his hands at a fire pit, the skin on the back on his neck prickled with the realization that he was being followed.

CHAPTER 4

Laguna Beach, California

THE MAN STOOD ABOUT THIRTY YARDS AWAY AT AN UNLIT FIRE PIT. He held a glass of beer and had just turned his back to Quinn, looking out to sea. In the dark, Quinn couldn't tell much. The man was of average height and build, wearing some sort of dark coat, jeans, and boots.

He had seen this man before. Just before he had opened the glass double doors to the beach walkway, the man had appeared at the other end of the long hallway, rounding the corner. The hallway had been dimly lit, but Quinn remembered the coat and the glass of beer.

He rubbed his hands together over the fire. Picking up his drink, he continued his stroll along the winding concrete walkway. When he reached the Studio, a small restaurant on the beach near the end of the property, he stopped and read the displayed menu. The man lingered farther down the walkway, as if deciding whether to go for a walk on the beach.

Quinn turned and walked back to the hotel, picking up his

pace. When he opened the double doors, the glass caught a shadowy reflection of the man, now less than twenty yards away, stopping to warm his hands at a fire pit.

No freaking doubt.

Quinn walked past the hall leading to the casino and took the elevator up to the Bistro, the intimate hotel bar. A scattering of couples chatted in the lounge. He sat at the bar and ordered a Glenfiddich on the rocks.

For the next two and a half hours, he stayed at the bar, chatting with the bartender, watching the sports reruns on the television monitors. He ordered another Glenfiddich, then another and another. During this time he made regular trips to the men's room, always carrying his drink with him. No one saw him when he poured each whiskey down the bathroom sink.

The bartender looked him over as he served him the fourth whiskey. Quinn's speech slurred. During his last trip to the men's room, his walk was unsteady, and he spilled a few drops of his drink.

By half past one, no other customers were left. Quinn took a cigar from his coat pocket, said good night to the bartender, and walked out of the bar, empty glass in one hand and cigar in the other.

To the right was a long hallway reaching to the far end of the property. Adjacent to the hall was a series of several small outdoor patios, each looking out to the sea, each with its own fire pit and patio furniture. Earlier in the evening, the patios had been full of people enjoying the blazing fires. Now the fire pits were cold, and the dark patios were deserted. All the outdoor lighting had been turned off to entice customers to visit the areas of the hotel that were still open.

Quinn opened the glass door of the farthest patio and sat down at a table in the chilly darkness. He unwrapped his cigar and, with some difficulty, lit it. As he smoked, he put his cell phone on the table and scrolled through the touch screen.

His lips pursed in frustration as he noticed his empty glass. He stood up, making sure to place his cell phone in the middle of the table, its blue screen set to glow at full brightness. Empty glass in hand, he left the patio and ambled down the hall toward the bar.

At the end of the hall he stopped, looking back to make sure he was alone in the hallway. Then, instead of going to the bar, he let himself into one of the other empty patios.

A few minutes later, a man wearing a black pea coat emerged from the stairway at the other end of the hall. The man scanned the hallway, then walked to the patio where Quinn had left his cell phone. He let himself in, took a quick look around, and snatched the glowing phone off the table.

Just as he did so, Quinn leaped forward from his crouch in the dark corner of the adjoining patio. He grabbed the man's wrist and slammed it hard against the edge of the patio table. The man grunted in pain, and the cell phone clattered to the floor. Quinn twisted the man's wrist up and behind his back in an elbow lock, bringing it up until the man doubled over. He shoved the man against the wrought-iron railing at the sea-edge of the patio.

The man grunted again but didn't speak. Keeping the pressure on the elbow lock, Quinn glanced around. No one was in sight. The other patios were deserted, and the fog limited visibility to a few feet. Since the hallway led only to the patios, the odds of someone approaching were remote.

With his free hand, Quinn patted the man down. No gun, no wallet, nothing. He leaned to the side and glimpsed a scarred face with bloodshot, drug-charged eyes.

The man looked like beach riffraff. He was about thirty and dressed all in black—a black pea coat, black jeans, and black

35

boots. The back of the balding head revealed a mottled scalp and scraggly hair.

A low-level operative. An addict with limited knowledge. The best results would come from appealing to the man's survival instinct.

Quinn wrenched the arm up until the man hissed in pain. The old policeman's hold still worked well. He leaned in to the man's ear.

"Hey badass."

The hunched figure was silent.

"Thought you had some hot stuff there with my phone? Now all you get is prison. Tell me who you're working for, and I might let you go."

The man said nothing.

Quinn jabbed his elbow hard into the man's kidney.

The man squealed in pain and coughed.

"Talk, badass, or I'll break your fingers."

The man muttered something unintelligible under his breath.

A patch of clouds had cleared, and in the moonlight Quinn saw sweat running down the balding back of the head and down the scrawny neck. The scraggly hair was wet, clinging to the scalp.

Quinn forced the man's arm up to the breaking point and leaned in to the scarred ear. "Louder, or they'll find your sorry ass in the dumpster tomorrow morning. Who are you working for?"

The man bent over farther, as if to mitigate the pain, his free hand dropping next to his boot. As he did so, he snarled in what sounded like Russian. "*Sookin syn.*"

The man ducked down. His free hand reached inside his boot while his locked arm pulled Quinn forward and off balance. With surprising speed, the man spun around, his free hand aiming at Quinn's throat.

The moonlight, the filtered light that had not existed a few minutes earlier, caught the flash of the steel blade. Quinn's arm blocked the knife thrust, but he had been pulled off balance and had let go of the man's arm. He fell forward, and the man's other arm came at him in a right cross.

He blocked the punch, took a step to regain his balance, and landed a quick jab to the face. The man grunted, but steel glinted in the moonlight as the knife came at Quinn a second time. He stopped it with a right uppercut that knocked the man's body off balance and toward the railing. As the man fell back, Quinn stepped forward and threw his entire body weight into a powerful left hook.

His fist hit the "sweet spot," the pressure point on the lower jaw below the corners of the lips. With the tremendous force of the blow, the man's head whipped violently to the side, and the man toppled backward over the railing and into the darkness.

CHAPTER 5

Laguna Beach, California

"SON OF A BITCH." THE FAMILIAR VOICE OF WILL, QUINN'S FIELD supervisor, crackled in his earpiece.

"Really?" Quinn swerved to pass a semi crawling along Pacific Coast Highway, then veered back into his lane before the oncoming minivan could honk at him.

"That's what that guy said before he went over the railing and met his maker. *Sookin syn* is a Russian phrase for an impolite reference to your lineage."

"And what do we know about this guy?"

"Not much, yet. Prints have him as a Russian national. Unemployed, a drifter. Lots of needle marks, but Interpol came back with no criminal history."

"How's this being handled?"

"We're cleaning it all up for you. Fortunately, there were no witnesses. The police will report it as an accidental fall, possibly a suicide. The hotel, of course, wants this all to go away as quickly as possible. We'll let you know if we find out anything more.

"That aside, we did some more digging on your new friend Marco. Turns out he's not as clean as he looks."

"How so?"

"When he was growing up in Italy, he was connected to the Societa Silenziosa, a mafia located in Calabria. Have you heard of them?"

"The Silent Society? They're a rough bunch. But here in the States, aren't they active only in New York?"

"They're expanding. They've introduced a new blend of heroin called "Snow White" that is spreading up and down the East Coast. The DEA is concerned."

"I thought Marco had no criminal record."

"He doesn't. Our sources say he bribed the Italian police to keep his record clean. Apparently he ended his association with the Society, though, when he started his pharmaceutical company. And he's been squeaky clean since he came to America." Will let out an exasperated sigh. "I think that's it for now. Anything you need?"

"The address of the man who sent this Russian after me."

"As do we, Michael. We don't need any more bodies in your wake. Next time remember to check for a knife in the guy's boot, okay? We'd prefer not to lose you. Whatever you are on to, somebody wants it bad." The call abruptly clicked off.

Frustration spreading up and down the chain of command. Not good. Who the hell was this Russian who had been following him? Was he connected to this Orlov?

The deadly late-night skirmish at the Montage had thrown a monkey wrench into what had been a promising evening. His fingers gripped the steering wheel. Sometimes he had to kill. He was hardened to it.

But, if he had to kill, he wanted to know damn well what it was *about*.

Enough. This meeting with Marco could be a game changer. He needed to be up for it. He drummed his fingers on the steering wheel as he turned off of Pacific Coast Highway for his first visit ever to the ultra-high-end community of Newport Shores.

The housing began as upscale tract homes, then proceeded up the economic ladder. By the time his GPS brought him to Coral Cove Lane, he was in an area of large custom homes. At the end of Coral Cove Lane was a private road with *No Exit* and *No Trespassing* signs. He ignored the silent warnings and continued on up the private road.

On both sides of the road was a man-made nature preserve, proclaiming the exclusivity of the grand estates ahead. One side was wetlands, with reeds and rushes. The other side was a forest, with willow and oak and eucalyptus trees. A wide dirt path, probably some sort of access road, led out from the forest to the private road.

About a half mile in, the road ended in a cul-de-sac with three concrete driveways, each shrouded in shrubbery with no signage. The driveway on the right led to Marco's Palazzo.

As he entered the driveway, he looked to his left, at the estate next to Marco's. He was surprised to see, beyond the six-foot stone wall that separated the properties, signs of serious disrepair. The adjacent property looked vacant. Roof tiles were cracked and crumbling. Weeds sprouted from a brown lawn. All of these useful observations were filed away in his mental hard drive.

In contrast, Marco's side of the driveway was a well-kept wall of solid dark green. Tall Italian cypresses, trimmed and planted as a hedge, protected Marco's property from intruding eyes.

Quinn came to a guardhouse and black wrought-iron gates. He gave his name to the guard. The guard gave him a sharp glance and checked his monitor. The gates opened, and the guard waved him inside

Aware that his every move was now being recorded on video, he scanned for anything that might prove useful.

There. A glint of sunlight revealed the secret. Buried in the back of the Italian cypresses was a black wrought-iron fence topped with sharp-edged finials. And on top of that fence was attached coil after coil of razor-edged concertina wire.

After a final winding turn, the driveway ended in a large cobblestone circle in front of the house. In the center of the circle, four verdigris mermaids holding pitchers fed jets of water into a bubbling fountain.

A uniformed valet greeted him and pointed toward the front entrance. As the valet drove his car away, Quinn paused to look up at the structure known in local society circles as the Palazzo al Mare, the Palace-by-the-Sea.

His eyes took in a soaring mansion with apricot-colored stucco walls, cream-and-gray stone trim, and curved balconies with elaborate white balustrades. The Mediterranean architecture, with its columns, arched windows, and grand portico, paid decorous tribute to the Old World. Majestic turrets curved out from the top left and right corners.

A smiling, gray-uniformed Filipino maid greeted him at the massive, white double-door entrance. She beckoned him into a stately foyer with curving staircases going up both sides. Gesturing for him to follow, she led him across the marble floor and down a wide hallway. He followed her past a large living room with a concert grand piano, and then the maid opened the French doors at the back of the house.

He stepped out into another world.

CHAPTER 6

Newport Shores, California

IT WAS A VISTA DESIGNED TO TAKE A FIRST-TIME VISITOR'S BREATH away. The entire rear grounds were carved on top of a sheer bluff, overlooking the Pacific Ocean sparkling in the mid-day sun.

Beyond the large, rectangular lawn was a free-form pool with an infinity edge facing out to sea. On the near side of the pool was an outdoor covered kitchen, bar, and dining area large enough for a small hotel, all done in slabs of black granite.

At the head of the granite dining table sat Marco, wearing sunglasses and talking into his cell phone's earpiece. He was dressed resort-style in a flowered camp shirt, khaki shorts, and sandals. Three dark-haired women in bikinis lounged on adjoining chairs, smoking and drinking brightly colored drinks. Quinn recognized the women from the previous evening at the Montage.

He followed the maid across the lawn to the dining area.

Marco was speaking in heated Italian, gesturing with his

free hand. As Quinn approached, Marco motioned for him to sit down and waved away the girls. He snapped his fingers at the maid, who nodded her head and retreated.

The three bikini-clad women, drinks and cigarettes in hand, sauntered off toward the chaise lounges on the opposite side of the pool.

Marco put down the phone and turned toward Quinn. A white smile flashed and disappeared.

"My apologies. Busy day. You are ready for lunch?"

"Yes, thanks. Nice place you have here."

A white-shirted waiter appeared. Marco ordered bottled water and a bottle of Pinot Grigio and told the waiter to bring the first course.

For a few minutes they discussed, as they had the previous evening at the Montage, the latest gossip of the art world. Quinn sensed he was again being vetted.

The waiter brought the water and wine. A second waiter came, bearing a plate of baked olives and another plate laden with small slices of artisan bread that had been grilled with goat cheese and roasted peppers. After the waiters left, the conversation continued while the men worked their way through the antipasto.

Marco smacked his lips as he swallowed the last bite of grilled bread. He sat back in his chair, removed his sunglasses, and looked at Quinn.

"You seem to be a man of discretion as well as expertise. I have a friend who may find your firm of assistance."

"How can I be of help?" Quinn's ears perked up at the mention of a "friend." He must have passed the vetting. The conversation was about to take a different turn.

Marco was silent while the waiters cleared away the first course.

As the waiters walked away, three men, all wearing dark T-shirts and slacks, approached the table.

Marco motioned to the middle man, presumably the leader. The man glanced at Quinn, then leaned over, cupped his hand, and whispered into Marco's ear. Marco nodded and dismissed the man with a wave of his hand.

As the three men walked away, the waiters reappeared with the next course, small bowls of spinach and tomato soup.

Marco tucked his white linen napkin into his shirt, making a bib. He sipped each spoonful of spinach and tomato soup, slurping in satisfaction.

"My friend," continued Marco between spoonfuls of soup, "is in possession of some rather valuable paintings. For some time the paintings have been in storage."

"I see."

"My friend, he inherited these paintings. He is not very familiar with the workings of the art world and is somewhat concerned about the provenance of these works. He wishes no trouble from the authorities. You understand, eh?"

"Yes."

"So, my friend has been advised to wait a specified period of years from the time he came into possession of the works. This waiting period, it is different for different paintings."

"I understand," said Quinn.

They were discussing, of course, how to move stolen art. The "waiting period" would be the statute of limitations on grand theft. The statutes would vary with different countries.

"When these waiting periods expire," Marco continued, "my friend may wish to dispose of some of these items. That is where your firm may be useful."

"We've helped many clients in similar situations."

"Some of these works, they are of great age. They may be missing proper documentation regarding their provenance.

Locating it would greatly facilitate the transactions. A firm such as yours can assist in finding such documentation?"

"Marco, my firm has the resources available to provide the appropriate pedigree for any work of art. Our firm welcomes the business of your friend." Quinn raised his wine glass. Hopefully he wasn't overplaying his hand. Mustn't appear too eager. He put calm professionalism into his tone. "*Salute.*"

"*Salute.*" Marco raised his wine glass.

The waiters cleared away the soup bowls and laid out the third course, a mushroom risotto.

So far, so good. Quinn sat back in his chair to make room for the waiters. He was looking out to sea when a loud crash, the sharp sound of china shattering on concrete, cut through the air. He turned his head back.

Marco's face was reddening as his upper lip curled into a sneer. His plate was in fragments on the patio, bits of rice everywhere, the splattered mushroom sauce forming tiny beige pools on the smooth concrete. The waiters came running over.

"Who made the risotto?" barked Marco.

"Arturo, *signore,*" replied the head waiter.

"Tell Arturo he is fired. *Immediatamente.* Tell him to clean out his things and leave. Tell him I said to go back to Italy and learn how to cook something as simple as risotto." With the edge of one hand, Marco tapped the palm of the other hand, then glared at the waiters. "Now bring the salmon. You think you can do that?"

"*Si, signore, si.*" The waiters were already on their hands and knees, cleaning up. In seconds they were gone.

Quinn kept quiet.

Marco looked over at him as if nothing had happened. "Very well, then. I will provide you with more information at a later time. You will await my orders."

Anger welled up inside Quinn's gut. Marco's dictatorial

manner was beginning to grate on his nerves. He forced a smile and nodded.

The waiters, acting as if they were about to genuflect to Marco, laid out the main dish.

The grilled salmon tasted of lemon and butter and basil and was so tender that just the touch of Quinn's fork sliced through it.

Marco ate in silence. The sulk after the tantrum.

To the side there was a soft, wet sound, the splash of someone diving into water. Quinn looked over at the free-form pool. No one was in the pool, and the three women were still lying on chaises, chatting and smoking cigarettes.

The splashing sound came again. He turned to look behind him. Someone was swimming in a second, much smaller pool, a two-lane lap pool near the side of the house.

"Ah," said Marco, "there she is."

Quinn glimpsed white and tan as a feminine figure executed a flawless flip turn. Halfway across the pool, the swimmer surfaced doing a smooth crawl, her tanned body cutting through the water like a knife through butter.

Marco's previous good mood seemed to be returning. After a final forkful of grilled salmon, he licked his lips and sat back in his chair. He wiped his hand across his mouth and gestured at what lay before him.

"Beautiful women, the best food, the best view, the best everything. This is what life is all about, eh?"

"Absolutely." Quinn forced a smile. His gut shuddered in repulsion. He loved the pleasures of life as much as anyone, but there was a Spartan side of him that rebelled when self-indulgence became decadence.

Another soft splash, and Quinn looked over to see the end of another smooth flip turn. This time the swimmer kicked all the way across underwater. She paused at the pool edge to breathe, and the sunlight sparkled on a wet mane of golden blonde hair.

"*Cara mia!*" Marco turned to the side and shouted. He clapped twice, then beckoned with a crooked finger. "*Vieni qui!* You are just in time for dessert and coffee."

In one motion, the woman pulled herself out of the water and onto the pool deck.

Sienna.

She wore a white string bikini, the white of freshly fallen snow, and the fabric clung as if it had been designed for her body. The halter top revealed a tantalizing amount of cleavage, and the low-rise bottom showed a smooth, taut tummy in front and golden cheeks in back. As she stood and turned to face them, the double-string side ties bounced against her hips, scattering drops of water.

Quinn watched her, not wanting to turn his gaze away. From the corner of his eye, he noticed Marco doing the same.

Sienna glanced shyly at the men at the table, waved in acknowledgement, and took a few steps over to the lawn, where she removed a comb from a beach bag. Arching her back and tilting her head back, her long legs apart, she let the sun dry her body while she combed out her mane of wet hair.

Beads of water glistened like diamonds as the sun shone on her shoulders and the upper part of her breasts protruding from the white bikini top. The gentle curves below her waist, coming together at the small of her back just above the firm buttocks, were exquisite. Her toned, tan body, posed like a statue of a Roman goddess with the blue sky as a backdrop, was stunning.

At the Montage the previous night, Quinn had been mesmerized by her eyes. Now, he decided, he would have to give equal regard to the rest of her.

The waiters cleared away the dishes and laid out fresh table settings for dessert for three.

Marco turned his gaze back toward Quinn. "You will have a tour of the Palazzo, and then you will be allowed a tour of my private gallery. There is much to show you. We can get back to business later." The appearance of Sienna had replaced his sulk with a look of smug self-satisfaction.

"Sounds great," Quinn replied, ignoring the disregard for whatever his plans might be. Great for intelligence gathering, and great as a way to keep appealing to Marco's endless vanity.

Sienna appeared at their table, wearing a translucent, white cotton cover-up over her bikini. A waiter pulled out her chair. She sat down gracefully.

"*Buon pomerrigio, mia donna,*" said Marco.

"*Buon pomerrigio,*" replied the girl, somewhat formally, glancing at both men. Quinn, surprised, sensed resistance from her to Marco's possessive familiarity.

The waiters laid out cups of rich, dark espresso and a platter of Italian cheeses garnished with strawberries.

"*Ascoltami.*" Marco beckoned Sienna with a crooked finger and, when she leaned over, proceeded to ignore Quinn and whisper in Sienna's ear. Sienna's eyes looked down as she listened.

As he waited, Quinn's mind processed the data it had collected so far. The pieces that made Marco were coming together like a jigsaw puzzle.

Marco fancied himself a monarch, a self-anointed king presiding over his royal court. They were updated for the twenty-first century, but the traditions of European royalty were there.

The man in black who had whispered into Marco's ear was the *majordomo*, the only member of the court allowed to approach the ruler in such a manner. The two men accompanying the *majordomo* were minions. The waiters and maids were sycophantic lackeys. And all around were armed bodyguards, who roamed the grounds and accompanied Marco on trips.

And Quinn himself? He had now been relegated to the role of a mere tradesman, a merchant with certain skills that would be useful to expand the monarch's wealth. As soon as he had agreed to do business with Marco, the man's attitude had changed to one of thinly veiled contempt. The veneer of civility could not mask the impression that Marco now thought he had Quinn in his back pocket, bought and paid for. Ready, like the rest of the entourage, to do the ruler's bidding.

On a deeper level, Quinn also sensed a disdain for human life itself. To someone like Marco, the humble humans around him were not much better than beasts of burden, useful only for their services.

He glanced over at the three women by the pool. Modern-day, royal concubines attracted to join the harem by the luxurious lifestyle and by the munificence of the monarch.

And Sienna? Following another tradition of European royalty, she would be the "declared mistress", the one woman above all others, to be treated with special respect and deference. Thus the separate, formal introduction the previous evening. And, of all the concubines, only the declared mistress would be given the royal perquisite to dine with the ruler.

Did she know that she was only one in a long series?

As if in answer, her eyes met his, then she averted her gaze. Marco finished whispering into her ear and patted her on the cheek. He sat back in his chair and turned toward Quinn.

"We were just discussing the upcoming Burns and Harriman art auction in Rome next week. I have previous commitments, so I am sending Sienna to bid on a few items. Your firm will be sending a representative?"

"Yes, absolutely," Quinn replied without skipping a beat. "As a matter of fact, I will be representing them at the auction." Somehow he would get this by Will. And it would give him a chance to look up a friend, Piero, his contact in Italy.

"Excellent. There are a few things you can work on for me while you are there."

Quinn smiled, gritting his teeth at the command. To his right, the three men in dark clothing were again approaching the table.

The *majordomo* carried a cell phone, and his brow was furrowed. He stood a few feet away and gestured, then made hand signals and pointed to the phone.

"You must forgive me." Marco stood, giving his table guests a cursory glance. "I have important business matters that require my immediate attention." He dropped his napkin on his plate and stepped back, pushing his chair away. "The tour of my gallery will wait for another day. Sienna will be happy to give you a brief tour of the grounds before you leave." Without waiting for a reply, he turned and strode off toward the Palazzo, whispering in Italian to the three men.

He was about a half-dozen steps away when he paused and looked back at the table.

"Oh, and you must come to my Midsummer Night's Dream party next month. I will send you the invitation." The deep-set eyes were those of a shark eyeing potential prey.

"You will have the time of your life, Mr. Quinn."

CHAPTER 7

Newport Shores, California

THERE WERE A FEW SECONDS OF AWKWARD SILENCE AS THE TWO
sat alone at the table. A fantasy crossed Quinn's mind, of he and
Sienna going for a swim in the pool, then ducking into one of
the upstairs guest bedrooms. He cleared the thought away, put a
polite smile on his face, and pushed his chair back.

Sienna stood and put on her sunglasses. "You've already
seen the back yard, no? Then I will show you the rest of the
grounds and the main floor. Please, you follow me." She turned
around and walked in the direction of the lap pool.

Her Italian accent had a charming softness to it, and Quinn
pondered its origin as he followed the golden legs and mane of
wet hair around the side of the house.

Past the lap pool was a well-kept formal garden. Sienna
slowed her step as she pointed out the various types of
flowers. Quinn pretended to be interested as he noted that the
wall of Italian cypresses, with its hidden fencing and razor
wire, started as soon as the bluff ended. Other than the

entrance road, the only access to the property would be to either climb up the sheer cliff to the back yard or somehow make it over the razor wire and fences surrounding the rest of the property.

The lion had chosen his lair wisely.

After the formal garden came a koi pond, then a maze of well-trimmed hedgerows. They turned a corner, and were at the front grounds. Sienna led him across the cobblestone driveway and into the foyer. Once inside, she removed her sunglasses, turned to check that Quinn was still following, and continued to walk ahead, avoiding eye contact.

Sienna led him on a brief and perfunctory tour, like a White House tour guide, of the public areas—living room, dining room, and restaurant-sized kitchen—on the first floor. From the kitchen, a door led downstairs to a cavernous underground garage. Why would the tour go down there? Then Quinn realized Marco wanted to show off his car collection.

On a spotless, white tile floor, lit by recessed ceiling lights, was a luxury car collector's dream. A white Bentley Continental Supersports shone next to a steel-gray Rolls Royce Ghost, followed by a red Ferrari 599 GTB. Altogether Quinn counted fourteen cars, all in showroom condition. Beyond the last car stood another gleaming group—a half-dozen high-end motorcycles. Quinn recognized a bright red Ducati Panigale and a black-and-yellow BMW S1000.

"He likes the *motocicletta* as well, I take it."

"Oh yes." Sienna stopped and pointed to some framed pictures on the wall above the bikes. "He used to race. I think those are pictures of the Italian—how do you say it? —Grand Prix."

She had stepped close to him to point out the pictures. Through the translucent fabric of her cover-up, her white bikini looked tantalizingly like a white bra and panties. The cover-up clung to wet spots where she hadn't quite dried herself off. Quinn breathed in the fresh scent of her damp hair.

Beyond the motorcycles was a fully equipped repair bay, complete with hydraulic lift. At the end of the garage, in the center of an empty gray wall, was a white door marked 'Exit'.

"What's beyond that?"

"Nothing," Sienna pronounced the word as "no thing." "Just the maintenance building and a side road."

"Well, we've come this far. We may as well complete the cook's tour." Quinn took a few steps toward the door and paused, turning back with a hopeful look.

Sienna's eyes were wide with bemusement, and her lips thrust out in a pout, as if to say, "Who would want to see that?" She sighed, shrugged her shoulders, and led him up a flight of concrete steps and out into the bright sunshine of the side yard.

Across the lawn was a two-story building that Quinn guessed housed the security headquarters on the second floor and the maintenance equipment on the ground floor. Beyond the maintenance building, close to the edge of the property, was the white concrete circle of an empty helipad. Beside it, partially hidden by the maintenance building, he could see the gray steel of a hangar.

"Marco does live large. No helicopter ride today?"

"It is, it is being worked on, I think you say." Sienna kept walking.

On the other side of the maintenance building, a small asphalt parking lot contained three black SUVs. From the parking lot, a short road led to a side gate. The wall of Italian cypresses stopped a few feet short of both sides of the side gate, leaving the ends of the black fence, and the ugly concertina wire on top, exposed in the sunlight.

Quinn looked at the side road. It simply looped around to the main driveway, the only way in or out of the property.

He turned around and glanced up at the second story of the main house and the turret that jutted out from the corner.

"Is that the guest wing?"

"Ah, no. The guest wing, it is on the other side, where we had lunch, yes? That up there—" she shielded her eyes from the sun as she looked up, and as she did so her breasts pressed against the thin fabric of the cover-up "—is Marco's private art gallery. No one is allowed in there without Marco." She put her hand down and looked at Quinn.

"Of course."

He was about to thank Sienna for the tour when a door from the side of the house opened. Two men, conversing in Italian, emerged from the doorway. Each man wore a black T-shirt and carried a rifle case. Quinn looked at the rifle cases and then up, noting that the turret was above the doorway.

Around the corner from the back of the house came two more men in black T-shirts, also chatting in Italian and each carrying a rifle case.

One of these two men had white bandages covering almost half his face and both of his forearms, and walked at a slower pace.

The two pairs of men fell silent and looked down at the ground as soon as they noticed they were not alone. The pair leaving the building passed the pair entering without so much as a nod.

Quinn looked at Sienna, eyebrows raised.

"It's just the guards." She shrugged. "Changing shifts, you call it?"

"I see." Quinn watched as the door closed and the men disappeared from sight. "What happened to that poor fellow with the bandages?"

"Oh, him. I think he had some sort of accident with the *chimici*, what you call the, the pool chemicals."

"Good to see he's on the mend. When did that happen?"

Sienna put a hand on her hip and bit her lip. "I think about two weeks ago. I believe he was, for a few days, in the hospital." She looked at Quinn. "Why?"

Quinn thought of the photographs of Blackwell's acid-tortured body. *Got you, Marco, you bastard.* "Oh, nothing. Just good to see him up and around. A similar thing happened to a friend once, and he was out for quite a while."

Time to go. He took a step toward the front entrance, then turned and extended his hand. "Sienna, I've taken enough of your time. I'll see my way out to the front and find the valet. I guess I'll see you in Rome?"

The remark gave Sienna pause. She took a step forward, her eyes appraising Quinn, as if noticing him for the first time. Her aloof tour-guide countenance melted away, replaced by a shy smile.

"Why, yes, *a Roma.*" She clasped his hand. "I guess you will."

CHAPTER 8

San Alessandro d'Aspromonte, Calabria, Italy

"THAT BUILDING IS *INESPUGNABILE*, MY FRIEND. IMPREGNABLE."

Piero Angellini, Quinn's contact in Italy, put down his night vision binoculars. He looked over and sighed. "There is no way we are getting in there."

Quinn put down his binoculars and rubbed his eyes. His shirt and pants were clammy with dried sweat and sticking to his skin. They had been lying in the dirt, watching the factory, since morning. Now it was almost midnight, and the stars shone quietly in the chilly darkness.

"*Pazienza*, Piero. Nothing is completely impregnable." He looked at the affable Italian next to him. "The graveyard shift is due to take over. Let's see what happens."

Piero grunted and picked up his binoculars.

Quinn had been granted permission to fly to Italy early, before the art auction in Rome, to allow a day for the reconnaissance of Marco's pharmaceutical factory. Coming to

Italy early had paid a dividend, a chance to catch up with an old friend. Was it four years ago he had first met Piero?

He refocused his binoculars. The object of their surveillance lay a few hundred yards beyond the knoll where they were camped. The building was quite telling in its anonymity.

The structure was squat and ugly. The two-story concrete box, surrounded by a barbed-wire fence with alarm horns, reminded Quinn of a prison. No sign or logo was evident. The building sat alone in a rural area miles from the nearest town, in the middle of acres of vacant land.

As if it didn't want to be noticed. Visitors were unwelcome.

The only access to the building was a road that led about a quarter mile out to the two-lane highway. Near the factory entrance, a guardhouse with chain link gates straddled the road. Quinn's binoculars had picked up the AK-47s the guards were carrying in addition to their holstered side arms.

He looked at the structure. It was said one could never really leave the mafia. And the Silent Society was close-knit. What was Marco up to in that building?

Two men approached the guardhouse, waving at the two men leaving. The graveyard shift had arrived.

In addition to their AK-47s, the two new guards were each carrying large, powerful-looking flashlights. At the entrance to the guardhouse, the men stopped and turned on their flashlights.

"Down." Quinn barely got the whisper out before his face hit the dirt. Both men lay still, hoping the knoll would hide their presence.

The harsh halogen beams swept the ground around them, lighting every rock and twig. From the corner of his eye, Quinn watched the light sweep the copse of trees where they had hidden Piero's Fiat. Would a telltale glint of metal give them away? He held his breath as the light paused at the trees.

Then the twin light beams moved on, making their way around the rest of the property perimeter. Finally the lights went out, and Quinn heard the guardhouse door close. He waited an extra minute before giving Piero the signal to resume their recon.

A pang in Quinn's stomach told him it was also time to get something to eat. He reached over to his backpack and extracted a bottle of water and two energy bars.

"How can you eat that stuff?" Piero watched Quinn unwrap the first bar.

"The same way I did for breakfast on the plane from Rome." Quinn chewed the bite, trying to make it last. "The apple cinnamon bar is the main course, and the chocolate crisp bar will be for dessert."

"My friend, before this is over, I need to take you out to dinner for some good Italian food." Piero looked with genuine pity at Quinn's half-eaten bar. "The last time I saw you, Michael, was two years ago when you were following that *molo* from Paris to Venice. You were eating the same *rifiuti* then, and I promised to show you that one can eat real food when on the job. But all we had time for at the end was to go out for a late-night drink. Remember?"

"How could I forget? You never did tell me how you found those two women."

"You didn't ask."

Quinn gazed at the building as he finished the last bite of his energy bar. "You know, Piero, if I ever do get married, maybe it should be, as you always say, to a nice Italian girl."

"That depends on how nice you want her to be."

There followed a discussion of the merits of women around the world, including a detailed description of their physical characteristics. Quinn was bringing up some distant memories of a member of the Brazilian women's beach volleyball team he had met on a trip to Rio during Carnival when something moved in his night-vision binoculars.

"Hold on," he whispered. "Look over to the left. The back of the parking lot."

At the far end of the lot, a truck was backing up. It stopped and idled in a dark corner. A second truck then backed up, lining up behind the first. Then a third truck. With the first truck leading the way, the three vehicles wound their way around the building and toward the guard gate.

"No lights," whispered Piero.

The gate swung open as the trucks approached. The guards remained in the guardhouse. As the trucks continued on the road leading to the highway, Quinn kept his binoculars trained on the back of the lead truck.

When the trucks turned left onto the highway, they each turned on their lights. He watched as the headlights of the second truck lit up the back end of the lead truck.

"And no license plates," Quinn whispered. "It's show time. Let's go."

PIERO GUNNED THE FIAT DOWN THE DIRT ACCESS ROAD AND ONTO the highway. Soon the red taillights of the rear truck shone in front of them.

"Got'em." Piero's hand tapped the steering wheel.

"With no license plates, aren't they concerned about being stopped by the police?" Quinn checked the action on his HK 9mm.

"The *carabinieri?*" Piero laughed. "In these parts, my friend, they are still a wholly owned subsidiary of organized crime."

"Looks like the lead truck is taking the next exit."

Piero downshifted into third as the pairs of red tail lights slanted off to the right. He glanced up at the exit sign.

"*La Porta*. They're headed to the port, Reggio Calabria."

Off the highway the traffic dwindled to a trickle, then vanished as they entered the deserted industrial section of the port town. Piero turned off the Fiat's headlights and followed the red taillights of the trucks through a twisting and turning series of narrow streets. The vague black shapes of warehouses and decrepit-looking buildings loomed around them. Through the open window, the cool night air smelled salty.

"They're headed right for the commercial harbor." Piero downshifted again.

The Fiat rounded a corner and into darkness. The red taillights were gone.

Piero banged the steering wheel and cursed in Italian.

"They're still there," said Quinn, looking through his night-vision binoculars. "They just turned off their lights for the last few streets. They're a block ahead. And they've slowed down."

The Fiat slowed as well, following the trucks. The briny odor of the commercial wharf filled the inside of the car.

"There. They're pulling up right on the dock." Quinn pointed. "Ahead and to the right, see those black shapes? This is close enough. Pull over at the end of this alley and kill the engine. We can watch them from the car."

The green-hued images showed the three trucks lined up parallel to one another, their cabs facing away from the water. Behind the trucks loomed the massive bulk of a freighter, moored in its berth. Beyond the ship, the binoculars picked up the calm green-and-white ripples of the Strait of Messina, quiet at this late hour.

To the right of the trucks, a metal ramp reached down from the ship to the dock. The driver of the first truck climbed out of his cab, waved at a man coming down the ramp, and opened the doors to the back of his truck. More men appeared from the ship and took up positions in a line down the ramp.

"No lights, no cranes," whispered Piero.

"They're doing this the old-fashioned way," replied Quinn. "A human chain. Simple and quiet."

Rectangular packages passed from the first truck up the chain of longshoremen. From there they would be hidden in one of the shipping containers on board.

"Looks like your hunch was right." Piero peered through the binoculars. "That's not sugar in those bricks. But if that's the stuff you want to see, and they're being that careful, how are we going to get a piece of it?"

Quinn was silent. He had his binoculars trained on the driver of the first truck. The driver disappeared inside the back of his truck, then came out and walked back toward his cab.

"There." Quinn pointed. "Look at the bulge in his jacket."

As the driver opened the door to his cab and climbed in, the shape of a rectangle bulged in front of his stomach.

"That's how we'll get a piece. That driver is taking home a brick for himself."

"He's risking his life." Piero frowned. "Then again, if that stuff is what you think it is, one of those bricks is worth more than what that driver makes in a year."

The first truck was now empty, and the longshoremen were unloading the second truck. The driver of the first truck climbed down from his cab. His jacket no longer bulged.. He joined the line passing bricks from the second truck up the human chain. Quinn was surprised at how quickly the operation was proceeding.

Time was running out. Just how was he going to get a sample?

All of the obvious options— following the trucks back, somehow separating the one truck from the others, then approaching the cab with guns drawn—were dangerous. And they would soon be back on the highway. The tiny Fiat would crumple like a tin can if it tried to force the big truck off the road.

"Piero, your tool kit."

"Right here." Piero reached behind and pulled a leather briefcase from the back seat.

Quinn opened the briefcase and found a packed to-go kit for the meticulous burglar—two kinds of slim jims, a hammer, knives, screwdrivers, rubber gloves, even a battery-operated drill.

"I'm going to go for it now, while they're occupied. The driver's dome light is turned off. They won't see me. I'll go in the passenger door and be back in five minutes." Quinn selected the long slim jim.

"Do not take any longer, my friend." Piero's whisper was tense.

The darkened docks stank of fuel and rotting garbage. Quinn picked his way past stacked fifty-gallon drums and wood pallets with cargo netting piled on top. The three trucks were parked several yards apart, enough distance so that the noise of the longshoremen working would mask the sound of the door lock. He ducked down and scrambled over to the passenger side of the first truck.

The hood said the truck was an Iveco. The vehicle looked to be about ten years old, with no sign of any alarm system. Quinn crouched next to the passenger door and tried the slim jim.

Hook end down, the thin piece of metal slid down between the window and the door. When it met resistance, he slid the metal from side to side, trying to find the lock-unlock bar. Once, twice, side to side, nothing.

He was moving the slim jim too fast. This time he dragged

the metal. Now the hook grabbed something. He gave a quick upward pull, and the lock button popped up.

The inside of the cab smelled of sweat and beer and was littered with fast food wrappers. Quinn found the plastic-wrapped brick of white powder wrapped in a newspaper and tucked underneath the passenger seat.

With a knife he cut a tiny slit in the bag, emptied a spoonful of the powder into a plastic bag, and tied the bag shut. He put the brick back, closed the door, and risked a look over the hood.

The longshoremen were finishing up with the last truck. Quinn gauged the distance to the alley and jogged back, trying to retrace his steps.

The darkness hid the cargo netting that hung down from the pallets to the dock. His left foot tangled in the netting and he stumbled, knocking over a half-dozen of the stacked fifty-gallon drums. The empty drums clattered to the dock and rolled every which way.

Quinn recovered his footing and ran toward the alley, but already angry shouts came from the longshoremen and flashlight beams scanned the area. One of the beams caught him, and a bullet zinged past him, clanging into one of the steel warehouses that fronted the alley.

Quinn zig-zagged the last few yards to the alley. As he rounded the corner, the Fiat started up and the passenger door opened. Behind him another bullet clanged into the warehouse. The shouts sounded much closer. "Turn around! Go the other way!" he yelled as he dove into the passenger seat.

Piero jammed the Fiat into reverse, knocking over a group of garbage cans, then shot forward toward the other end of the alley.

Quinn drew his 9mm and looked at the shadowy human shapes behind them, preparing to lay fire.

Piero shouted something, and Quinn looked ahead. Above the whine of the Fiat, he heard a deeper engine noise.

A large black shape moved across the end of the alley.

"One of the trucks," Piero yelled. "Going to block our exit!"

Quinn was already leaning out of the passenger window. He aimed his 9mm at the truck cab. He could see the driver's arm sticking out, holding a pistol. Quinn adjusted his aim and fired three times in quick succession.

The driver's arm jerked back inside, and the truck veered to the side. Metal-on-metal screeched as the hood and fender crumpled against the warehouse. The truck stopped in its tracks, its engine idling.

Quinn fired two more rounds, shattering the truck's windshield as they raced past.

Then the Fiat was out of the alley, rocketing through the twisting narrow streets. In seconds they were back on the highway.

Piero shouted a string of Italian curses, then took a deep breath and looked in the rear view mirror. He took another deep breath as he changed lanes and slowed the Fiat down to the speed limit. "No way they can chase us in those slow trucks."

"Messy, but we got it done." Quinn looked at the plastic bag in his hand. "My guess is they'll think we were locals who saw a crime of opportunity. They'll have their hands full getting out of there, not to mention dealing with the driver who stole from them."

"And they certainly won't be going to the police." Piero checked his rear view mirror. "Just the same, Michael, let's get you to your plane and back to Rome. I believe you have a meeting with a young lady tomorrow."

CHAPTER 9

Rome, Italy

QUINN LEAFED THROUGH HIS AUCTION CATALOG, DOING HIS BEST to look nonchalant as he waited in the quiet foyer of the Burns and Harriman building.

His research on art history had proven, unexpectedly, fascinating. From the night some lonely prehistoric soul was driven to paint, on a cave wall in Lascaux, pictures of the animals he hunted by day, art had been a way for mankind to understand the world. A way that predated writing, and even speech.

In the great room next door, immensely valuable artworks were being auctioned off to bidders from around the globe. Quinn put the scene out of his mind and focused on his mission. His goal for the evening was to get some time alone with Sienna and find out what she knew about Marco.

But how to do this and make it look like happenstance?

The two security guards in the foyer listened as a burst of applause came from inside the auction room, followed by the excited buzz of the crowd. The auction had ended. The double doors opened, and the guests—middle-aged and dressed in business attire or formal wear—streamed out.

Quinn waited in the foyer and pretended to look at his auction catalog. When Sienna emerged, he took a step toward her and smiled as if he had just happened to notice her.

"Michael!"

He had expected the indifferent tour guide from the Palazzo. Instead, she walked right over to him.

She looked elegant in a sleeveless, cream-colored, pleated lace dress. Her body scent, a mix of oranges and almonds, teased his senses. They shook hands, and his skin tingled when she left her hand clasped in his.

Then her cheeks flushed in self-awareness, and she withdrew her hand and let it fall to her side. "I mean, Mr. Quinn. Sorry."

"Please, call me Michael. How about some fresh air, after three hours in that stuffy room?"

"Ah! That would be nice. Just one moment."

Sienna stepped away and whispered to a heavyset man in a black suit standing behind her. The man nodded his head and gave Quinn a sharp glance as she walked back. "That was my bodyguard." She smiled. "Marco won't let me go anywhere without one. I told him to take a break, that I would be safe with you."

Quinn led her through the crowd, and the heavy brass doors of the Burns and Harriman building opened onto the wide boulevard of Via Fontana in the heart of downtown Rome.

With Sienna at his side, he stopped on the sidewalk and looked around.

The cool night air was refreshing, but the busy street was a cacophony of lights and noise.

To his right, a few doors down, was a restaurant with a

covered outdoor patio. It looked like an island of tranquility amid the noise of the boulevard. Most of the tables were empty, and the well-dressed waiters talked quietly among themselves. Both sights were signs that the restaurant was high-end and a quiet place to talk.

He touched Sienna's elbow. "How about something to eat or drink?"

"Both sound great."

Quinn had the odd sensation that Sienna, who had been so standoffish before, now *wanted* to be with him.

He led her through the throng of tourists on the sidewalk and tipped the maître d' for a table with the best view of the boulevard. When they were seated, with the roof over them and the glass walls on three sides of the patio, the bustle of the crowds faded into the background.

Their waiter, presuming they were a vacationing or honeymooning couple, fussed over them as he set the table, lit the candles and, in respectable English, talked about the day's specialties. From the menu they ordered a bottle of Chianti and bruschetta with sun-dried tomatoes. Quinn kept the conversation to small talk as they enjoyed the full-bodied wine and the grilled tomatoes and bread.

With the sensual pleasures of the food and drink, Sienna seemed to relax. She giggled when the waiter said something to her in Italian as he poured her a second glass of wine. Leaning back in her chair, she stretched her long golden legs out from her lace dress.

The scent of oranges and almonds drifted over. Her body wash. He caught himself staring at her legs and thinking of her in her white bikini, emerging dripping wet from the blue water of the Palazzo swimming pool. He took a bite of bruschetta and shifted his gaze to her face. But her green eyes captivated him, so he looked at the long tresses of ash-blonde hair falling over her shoulders. Was her hair perhaps more of a honey-blonde?

The problem with a woman like Sienna was that if one looked at her at all, it required an effort *not* to stare. Behind him, his male sixth sense detected the waiters leering at her as they walked by.

He forced his mind to focus. The best way to get her to talk about Marco would be to get her to talk about herself.

"So, Sienna. I'm guessing you were an art student?"

"Yes." She stroked the outside of her wineglass. "Since I was little, I've loved art, drawing in particular. I grew up in a small town—well, a *villagio*, really—in southern Italy, maybe a hundred miles from the coast. The nearest big city is a *porto*, Reggio Calabria, it is called. You have heard of it?"

"Think so," replied Quinn. An image of Reggio Calabria from the night before, of the chaos at the filthy docks, popped up in his mind. The drug sample had been picked up from his hotel room in Rome soon after he had checked in. The sample of white powder was probably already somewhere over the chilly Atlantic, on its way to Dulles airport. "A *villagio* in rural Italy sounds like a wonderful place to live. I'd like to hear about what it was like growing up there."

"It was *tranquillo*," Sienna said. "My family ran a small produce market in the village. My father was full-blooded Italian, my mother French, so I grew up speaking a bit of French as well as Italian."

And that explains, thought Quinn, the charming softness of her speech, down to the soft *j* sounds and the liquid *r* sounds, as well as her ash-blonde hair.

"So, you were this little girl who liked to draw?"

"Ah! I loved it so. Among my earliest memories are drawing figures with my *pastelli*, my crayons. My parents were dear people who wanted the best for their only child, and so they sent me to a private school where I studied art."

"And you continued to draw in school?"

"Always. By high school my passion had become *di figura*, I think you say figure drawing? I have always been fascinated by the beauty of the naked human body, especially the female figure in *riposo*."

"I'd like to hear more about that."

Absorbed in her memories, Sienna toyed with a lock of her hair. "After high school I enrolled in a small arts college on the Italian coast. I also became a *modello figura*, what you call a figure model. I posed for local artists as well as fellow students. At first I was shy, I think you say, about posing without any clothes on." She ran a hand through her hair, and glanced down at her body. "But everyone was so *simpatico*, I soon learned to relax, to enjoy it."

Fleeting images of the girl posing for figure modeling crossed Quinn's mind. He was about to ask a question when a loud screech interrupted, followed by the grating noise of metal on metal, and then the tinkling sound of broken glass.

He sat up and scanned the boulevard. Near the entrance to the auction house, a delivery van was double-parked. A small pickup truck, not realizing the van had stopped, had slammed on its brakes to avoid a collision. The truck had then been rammed by the sedan behind it. The front fender of the sedan had crumpled up like tin foil, and the headlights of the sedan and the tail lights of the truck lay shattered in the street.

The drivers of both vehicles got out and began gesturing and arguing in heated Italian. A few passersby watched in amusement.

"That's a reminder not to drive in Rome." Quinn smiled, keeping an eye on the scene. "Now, where were we? You continued the modeling through college?"

"Ah, yes. My sophomore year I was accepted as an exchange student at the Ecole des Beaux-Arts, a famous arts school in France. You have heard of it? That was the happiest time of my life. I was free to pursue my passion for figure drawing. I hope someday I can return to it."

"Why not pursue it now?"

"Marco." She spoke the name as if it had a bad taste. Her green eyes flashed. "He would never allow it."

Quinn sensed an opening. "Then if it's your passion, why not leave? It's a free country."

Sienna gripped her wine glass. "I cannot leave. I—it is—ah, you would never understand."

"Try me. I promise to keep whatever you tell me a secret."

Sienna's eyes were wide, as if she had decided to bare her soul. She leaned forward, her voice a whisper. "Marco, he is still a powerful man in Calabria. He threatened my family if I—if I did not become his woman. *Pah!*" Her shoulders gave an involuntary shudder. "That is why there is a bodyguard, always. Marco, he fears I will escape."

A coughing noise from passersby on the sidewalk turned Quinn's attention back to the traffic accident. Smoke billowed from beneath the hood of the crashed sedan. The driver of the sedan had lifted the hood and seemed to be cursing at his radiator. The smoke spread toward the sidewalk.

The scene unfolding before him had all the telltale signs of a staged accident. Possibly it was mere insurance fraud. Possibly it was more.

Quinn reached for the 9mm in his small-of-back holster, and grimaced when he remembered that the auction security guards had required him to leave his gun in his room. Why hadn't he gone back after the auction and retrieved it? Damn! He needed to get Sienna back inside the building.

"Please, you must promise to forget everything I say." Sienna implored him. "I don't know why I—there's something about you—this might be the only —*Oh!*"

A blinding bright light flashed around them. Sienna shrieked. A thunderous *bang* knocked Quinn off his chair and sideways onto the sidewalk.

For a few moments, he lay stunned on the concrete.

Consciousness returned, and his body ached from head to toe. He blinked, but there was nothing but blackness.

He blinked again, and the blackness faded to a murky brown haze that swirled around him. His head began to throb. A faint roar sounded, somewhere in the distance.

He lifted his head and looked around. The brown haze was smoke everywhere around him, burning his eyes. He inhaled and coughed up the noxious smoke clogging his lungs.

His hearing returned, and the faint roar became a loud chorus of screams and shouts and car horns. He got to his hands and knees, coughing smoke out of his lungs, and waved his arm around to see though the smoke.

Their table lay on its side in front of him, the wine bottle, plates, and glasses in pieces on the sidewalk. The shattered wall of the restaurant littered the area with a thousand knife-sharp shards. His chair lay on its side near the table. A few feet beyond that, Sienna's chair lay on its back.

But there was no sign anywhere of Sienna.

He staggered to his feet and shouted her name. Through the commotion, a woman's faint voice cried his name. There. Through the smoke, two men in coveralls were dragging Sienna across the asphalt, toward the back doors of the double-parked delivery van. Cursing, he sprinted full force toward them.

When Quinn reached the van, the men had turned their backs to him in order to open the van doors. The man on the right was closest. Without breaking speed, Quinn tackled the man around the neck and slammed the man's face against the edge of the open van door.

The man squealed in pain and let go of Sienna.

Quinn wrenched the man's head down hard, shoving the man's face into the metal rear bumper. The impact made a fleshy, crunching sound, and blood splattered onto the bumper and the back of the van. The man slumped into a pile on the street.

The second man, hampered by holding on to Sienna, pulled a handgun out of his coverall pocket. Quinn grabbed the gun barrel with both hands and twisted it to the gunman's right with so much force that the grip was ripped out of the man's hand. The man's trigger finger, trapped in the finger guard, broke with a faint but audible snap.

The man screamed as the gun slipped off his trigger finger and clattered to the street. Quinn brought his right elbow up, full force, into the underside of the man's chin. The man staggered back but still managed to hold on to Sienna.

Quinn grabbed the man's head with both hands and shoved his face hard onto his knee, then wrenched the head sideways.

The man let go of Sienna and crumpled onto the asphalt, his neck at an odd angle and the streetlamp shining on the bright red blood streaming down his face.

Quinn turned around and cradled Sienna in his arms. Her body trembled, and her breath came in short gasps. Large patches of blood streaked her legs, and parts of her dress were shredded from being dragged across the asphalt and broken glass. The right shoulder strap had been ripped away, and her right shoulder was covered in oozing blood.

He wiped the blood away, looking for the wound, when the orange-and-white *ambulanza,* its triple horn blaring, pulled up alongside them.

CHAPTER 10

Rome, Italy

THE PALE LIGHT OF A MIDNIGHT MOON STREAMED IN FROM THE balcony, illuminating the nightly gift laid out by the hotel staff: two white cotton bathrobes draped over the gold damask armchairs, two crystal glasses, and a silver ice bucket containing a chilled bottle of Clos du Mesnil champagne.

Quinn stared at the arrangement with contempt. Sitting on the gold damask couch facing the armchairs, wearing only a towel wrapped around his waist, he was still wet from his shower. He looked down at his ringing cell phone in his hand and typed in the encryption code. He glanced at the half-empty whiskey bottle and solitary glass on the table in front of him and wondered how that consumption was going to mix with the double dose of sleeping pills he had just taken.

"Will, you sound like you're on a raft floating in the middle of the Atlantic."

"Sorry, Michael. Something to do with the encryption algorithm. Got some intel on what happened today."

"How's the girl?"

"She'll be fine. Superficial injuries only—a lot of cuts on her body from being dragged across the asphalt. As soon as she was released from the emergency room, her, ah, employer, Mr. Leone, had a police escort take her to the airport and put her on a nonstop to California."

"And the men from the van?"

"Identified. Both Russian nationals. Passports in good order, and nothing came up on Interpol. Who knows what they did inside Russia, obviously. They were in Italy on tourist visas."

"Did they talk? Any connection between them and this Orlov?"

"No link so far. But again, Russia is its own world. And they never got the chance to talk. One died on the way to the hospital, the other shortly after arriving in the emergency room. It's just as well. The Italian police are cooperating and don't need any loose ends. The story in the media tomorrow will be an attempted robbery of a wealthy auction patron, a patron who wishes to remain anonymous."

"Anything from the scene?"

"So far it looks like it went down as you thought. A combination of smoke grenades and a hell of a stun grenade. The two Italian drivers vanished, of course, during all the turmoil."

"Thanks, Will. Anything else?"

"Yes. You're lucky you're not in the hospital. You might be more shaken up than you think. Get some rest."

"That's already been taken care of." Quinn's speech slurred. The sleeping pills were kicking in. His vision began to blur as he signed off.

He made his way to the white marble bathroom where he brushed his teeth, splashed water on his face, and stared at his bleary reflection in the gold-framed mirror. He felt the several small cuts near his jaw and cuts on the knuckles of both hands from the explosion and ensuing struggle.

What a fiasco. In one day, he had gone from being on top of the case to having it spin out of control.

His mind searched for the positive. Sienna was going to be okay. The two Russians were lowlifes who deserved to die a dozen times over. The story would be local news for a day, then would be replaced by the latest scandal.

Things would be better tomorrow. They had to be.

With the double dose of sleeping pills coursing through his veins, he moved from the bathroom to the bedroom. The hotel staff had turned down the yellow, floral silk bedspread and placed two chocolates on the pillows. He glanced at the gold sconces on either side of the upholstered burgundy velvet headboard and at the gold chandelier hanging from the coffered ceiling.

The whole effete scene looked ridiculous.

Quinn uttered a single curse word and threw his wet towel on the floor. Naked, he climbed into bed and pulled the bedspread over his body. He turned on his side, and in seconds was asleep.

The debris of the day, the chaos and the death, filtered through to his subconscious, producing restless sleep and troubled dreams.

He was swimming in some unknown black ocean in the middle of the night. The only sound was the splashing of his freestyle. In the distance, he heard Sienna's voice somewhere far ahead of him, faintly calling his name.

He lowered his head and swam a dozen quick strokes. He needed to catch up with her and find out what this was all about. But when he lifted his head to breathe, something had changed.

Before, the sea had been calm and quiet. Now a cold, wild

wind whipped the black water into angry turbulence. Whitecaps frothed and churned around him. Dark waves crashed into one another, sending showers of spray into the air. He tread water, trying to keep the salty spray out of his eyes. Sienna's voice called his name, fainter and fainter ...

Quinn awoke with a start and realized his arms had been treading water against sweat-soaked bed sheets. The voice was his ringing cell phone. The ceiling was a sea of yellow and white flashes. He blinked, fighting off the residue of the alcohol and sleeping pills. This time, when he opened his eyes, he could make out the gold chandelier hanging from the coffered white ceiling.

He threw off the yellow silk bedspread, sat up, and rubbed his eyes. The ringing cell phone was lying on the floor, its blue screen flashing next to his crumpled bath towel. He picked up the phone and punched in the encryption code. The display screen read 5:03 a.m.

"Good morning, Michael," said the cheery voice. "Called to let you know your flight is on time."

"Will, dammit, you called to tell me that?"

"And that it is an earlier flight, leaving in about two hours."

"Why?"

"Change of plans, Michael. You're coming back to California early. Looks like this mystery painting is on the move."

CHAPTER 11

The Palazzo Supremo Hotel, Rome, Italy

"MUDAK!"

Viktor Orlov shouted the Russian curse as the crystal glass flew through the air and shattered against the corner of the white wood mantel. Chips of glass and wood flew in all directions.

The two bodyguards ducked, then looked up at their superior.

"No more!"

The bodyguards ducked again, for this shout accompanied a heavy bottle flying over their heads. The bottle crashed against the center of the mantle, gouging out a fist-sized chunk of wood and shattering an eighteenth-century Italian porcelain vase which the hotel staff filled daily with red roses. The bodyguards stared as the debris rained down on the polished marble hearth, an odd-looking mix of broken glass and porcelain and roses lying in a pool of vodka.

Holding another vodka bottle in his hand, Viktor Orlov

walked from the bar to the small, wood writing desk that faced the balcony.

The laptop on the left displayed a video of a local Italian television news broadcast. The news anchor was recounting an attempted robbery that had occurred the previous evening near the entrance of the famed Burns and Harriman auction house. The robbery had resulted in some sort of explosion and the deaths of two innocent delivery men. The video behind the news anchor showed scenes of the aftermath, of wrecked cars and the charred patio of an adjacent restaurant.

"Two more of my men gone!"

The bottle of vodka in Orlov's hand swung down and struck the edge of the wood desk. Chunks of wood flew into the air, then fell on to the thick carpet. The small writing desk sagged to the right, but continued to stand.

Orlov turned his gaze to the laptop on the right. The screen displayed one picture, a photo of a glossy magazine cover. The magazine was called *Orange Coast Society*, and the cover featured a daytime photo of a dark-haired, Mediterranean-looking man wearing a white summer tuxedo. The man stood in front of an apricot-and-cream colored mansion with his arm around a pretty blonde woman. The caption of the cover photo read in bold white letters:

Orange Coast Society Art Patron of the Year
Marco Leone and friend at his Palazzo

Orlov spoke to the photograph. "*Svin'ya*, it seems our paths are destined to cross. I would have returned your girlfriend unharmed, as ransom for the art treasure that is rightfully mine. Now I must deal with you again."

He walked over to his hotel suite bar, filled a glass with ice cubes and poured the vodka over the ice. After consuming half of the drink in one swallow, he refilled the glass and turned and looked at the photograph.

"You seem somewhat accomplished, I will say. But even if you have heard of me, you have no understanding of what you are up against.

"Do you think you are grand, with your tuxedo and mansion? When your ancestors were peasants picking grapes, mine were *dvoryanstvo*, high nobility in the Great Russian Empire. We defended the Tsars against the separatist traitors and against the Communists.

"Do you think you are an art collector, with your little gallery? My family once had the largest collection of Fabergé, the greatest collection of Russian icons. Our vaults contained treasures that dwarfed the Crown Jewels.

"Your arrogance will lead me right to the greatest treasure of all. I am close now. I can feel it. I will get her back, and I will possess her forever.

"*Svin'ya*, enjoy your pretty girlfriend while you can. I will follow you to the gates of hell to recapture what is mine. Then I will slaughter you like the swine that you are." Orlov tapped the keyboard.

The magazine cover was replaced by another photograph, taken the previous evening, of the outdoor patio of the restaurant near the Burns and Harriman building. The photo had been cropped and enlarged to show a well-dressed, young couple sharing a bottle of wine and looking out at the boulevard. The woman, the same woman from the magazine cover, wore a cream-colored lace dress and smiled. The man was looking intensely at something in the street.

Orlov's face darkened as he looked at the man in the picture.

"And you, you foolish, ignorant *Amerikanskii*. Do not think I have forgotten you. You have no idea what you have gotten involved with. You have meddled in my affairs for the last time.

"When I am done with the others, I will come for you."

CHAPTER 12

Milan, Italy

AT THE BUSY MILAN AIRPORT, IN THE QUIETER SECTION RESERVED for private aircraft, one area was still. Gray-black clouds hung low in the afternoon sky, dampening any ambient sound. Only one aircraft, a shiny black Gulfstream V jet, was parked on the tarmac. The sleek plane sat dark and empty.

The stillness was broken by a convoy of three SUVs that pulled up alongside the Gulfstream. The doors of the still-dark jet opened and a built-in set of airstairs descended to the tarmac. With military precision, men emerged from the front and back SUVs, each man carrying an AK-47. The men positioned themselves around the plane so that all sides were guarded.

The uniformed flight crew—pilot, copilot, and attendant—exited the front SUV and jogged up the stairs and into the plane. Lights came on in the cockpit, and the roar of the jet's Rolls-Royce engines warming up drowned out the idling SUVs.

Four men emerged from the middle SUV. They were

carrying a rectangular metal object about the size of a large suitcase. The men carried the case up the airstairs and into the plane.

The noise of the jet engines increased as the airstairs ascended and the armed guards piled back into the SUVs. The wheels of the Gulfstream were already moving as the SUVs drove away.

The runway lights blinked on, bright in the afternoon gloom. The engines roared as the plane picked up speed, the navigation lights on the wings glowing red and green, the strobe lights at the front and back flashing a brilliant white.

The powerful engines lifted the jet up into a graceful climb, and in seconds the aircraft disappeared into the low-hanging clouds.

CHAPTER 13

Newport Shores, California

QUINN SHIVERED IN THE MORNING CHILL. IT WAS TIME FOR breakfast.

Lying on the rooftop of the vacant mansion, his head propped up on his backpack, he grabbed the bag of beef jerky next to him, opened it and selected the largest piece. Chewing the tough, salty meat, he watched a flock of seagulls flying out towards sea. Then he lay on his stomach, picked up his binoculars, and resumed his surveillance of the road that led to Marco's Palazzo.

As his plane was landing in California, Quinn had received a text informing him that Marco's Gulfstream V private jet had departed from Milan and was traveling nonstop to the Orange County airport. This was of particular interest because Marco was not on the plane. He had been spotted at his Palazzo in Newport Shores, as had Sienna.

The arrival of Marco's jet without Marco meant that the plane was bringing something of high importance.

A painting? Then it would need to be delivered, somehow, to Marco at his Palazzo.

Quinn had decided to stake out the Palazzo. As soon as his flight had landed, he had gone straight home, packed his backpack, and headed his BMW motorcycle toward the highway.

The roof of the vacant mansion adjacent to the Palazzo offered an ideal vantage point for a stakeout. The property had been empty for months. The previous owner had declared bankruptcy, then left the country and disappeared. Breaking into the house had been child's play.

On the rooftop, he had selected a chimney near a corner, equidistant from two sides, to set up camp. In one direction was the Palazzo with its long, winding driveway. In the other was the entire private road leading up to the Palazzo from the houses of Coral Cove Lane and the rest of Newport Shores. If anything was to be seen, it could be seen between these two endpoints.

And, unless a helicopter flew overhead, he could see without being seen. Behind him was the third of three estates at the end the private road, a stately white neo-Colonial whose owners, a retired couple, were away on vacation.

The first few hours of his late-afternoon stakeout had seen a few cars arrive at the residences down on Coral Cove Lane. Quinn had watched the cars pull into the driveways, and then lights come on in the upper floors.

Then night had fallen. A long, chilly night during which not one vehicle had entered or left on the private road. For whatever reason, Marco had decreed that no one from the Palazzo was allowed to leave or arrive before daylight.

Quinn shivered in the gray light of dawn. His watch read 6:19 a.m. He was reaching for another piece of jerky when the noise of multiple engines interrupted the quiet morning.

At first, he thought it might be the local gardeners with their trucks and leaf-blowers. Then he recognized the low rumble of a diesel engine.

He trained his binoculars on Coral Cove Lane. The rumble grew louder. A convoy of three vehicles traveled up the length of Coral Cove Lane and onto the private road.

The vehicles were headed toward the Palazzo.

He recognized the vehicles at the front and back of the convoy, with their tinted windows and all-terrain tires, as the black SUVs from the Palazzo's maintenance parking lot.

The vehicle in the middle had the diesel engine. It looked like a cross between a Brinks armored truck and a military assault vehicle. The body was painted a desert tan, and showed the rivets of thick armor plating. The windows were small and tinted black. On top of the rectangular roof was a smaller roof, raised up about two feet.

Quinn moved his AR-10 .308 sniper rifle into position, bracing the stock against his shoulder and settling into his cheek-weld. With his variable power scope he would be able to pinpoint any target on the road. His fingers felt the trigger guard.

The odd convoy was moving at about ten miles per hour. He looked at the middle vehicle. Despite its military appearance, it showed no artillery. Did it rely on the guards in the SUVs for defense?

His head jerked up from the riflescope at the sudden roar of other engines that drowned out the rumble of the convoy.

"Now!" yelled Viktor Orlov.

His four dark brown SUVs raced out from the wooded glen where they had been hiding. Clouds of dust billowed from the dirt access road as the vehicles shot onto the asphalt. The SUVS surrounded the convoy that had been making its way up the private road, blocking any escape.

The three-vehicle convoy stopped, its engines idling.

Orlov barked another order from his command post, the middle seat of the SUV blocking the front of the convoy.

His men, two exiting each SUV, took up positions around the convoy. All eight men were dressed in black, with black hoods, and were armed with AK-47s with high-capacity drum magazines.

"Fire!" yelled Orlov.

All eight men fired in unison at the three vehicles. The staccato *rat-tat-tat* echoed up and down the road as the AK-47s blasted hundreds of rounds at the convoy, firing at the driver's windows, then at the passenger windows, then at the vehicle doors and tires, until Orlov gave the order to stop.

He looked at the scene in stunned disbelief.

Windows should have been shattered, tires should have been flattened, and the occupants should have been either dead or dying. Yet the vehicles stayed in place, undamaged. As if they were waiting.

"Yuri!" Orlov shouted at his lead gunmen and pointed at the middle vehicle. The gunman jogged up to the driver's window and fired point-blank from his AK-47. He scrambled back as the bullets ricocheted off the bulletproof glass.

Orlov heard a mechanical hum as the top of the raised roof of the middle vehicle rolled open, followed by another hum as something rose up from inside the vehicle. He put his hand on the RPG, the rocket-propelled grenade launcher, which sat next to him on the car seat.

The armed men stepped back, their AK-47s raised in alarm. A glint of gray metal appeared at the top of the SUV.

Orlov cursed as he recognized the six rotating barrels of the machine gun—the extremely powerful, rapid-fire kind of machine gun used by the military to arm its helicopters and gunships. The deadly gun was being operated from inside the vehicle.

His hooded gunmen fired as the machine gun came into their view, but it was too late.

Bursts of yellow fire blazed from the six rotating barrels. A jackhammer-like noise echoed up and down the private road. The machine gun rotated 360 degrees, its remote operator aiming the barrels at the attackers.

The gunmen staggered backward, screaming as they were hit by the hail of bullets, their AK-47s jerking up in the air or clattering to the street.

In seconds, half of the gunmen were sprawled on the road— some trying to crawl, others still. The gunmen still standing fired their AK-47s again, desperately looking for a vulnerable part of the vehicle.

The machine gun continued on a second pass. The six rotating barrels blasted the gunmen laying in the street as well as those still standing. The bodies on the ground twitched as the barrage of bullets sliced through limbs and organs and splattered chunks of flesh onto the street. The gunmen still standing screamed anew as the second round of bullets slammed into them. One by one, they dropped their AK-47s and crumpled to the ground.

The jackhammer noise rattled the street until all of the bodies stopped moving. Then the machine gun ceased fire, and the only sound was the metallic pinging as the last spent rounds bounced off the vehicle and rolled onto the street. Then came silence.

Orlov's scream of rage broke the silence.

He opened the door on the far side of his SUV and climbed out, carrying his RPG launcher on his shoulder. He crouched and aimed the rocket launcher across the hood of the SUV, at the driver's window of the assault vehicle. Nothing could withstand this. He shouted as he pulled the trigger.

But the six barrels of the machine gun fired first.

The fusillade caught Orlov in the split second between the brain sending instructions to fire and the finger pulling the trigger. His RPG launcher was wrenched to the side. The warhead launched towards the sidewalk on the other side of the road. A *boom* and a streak of white smoke, and chunks of concrete from the sidewalk flew into the air.

The machine gun ceased fire. Orlov staggered sideways, still holding on to the rocket launcher, looking at the explosion across the street.

The machine gun erupted again.

Now Orlov did an odd sort of dance as the hundreds of rounds jerked his body in all directions. The rocket launcher flew out of his hands and bounced onto the street. Then the jackhammer noise ended.

Orlov's mangled body collapsed onto the asphalt and lay still. Pools of blood oozed out, glinting red as the first rays of morning sun emerged from behind the gray clouds.

For several seconds the street was quiet. Then the silence was broken again, this time by the wail of distant police sirens.

CHAPTER 14

Newport Shores, California

HONEY-GOLD RAYS OF LATE-AFTERNOON SUN SHONE THROUGH the windows of what had once been the vacant mansion's library. Refracting through the beveled glass, the rays flecked mottled shadows on the opposite wall.

Quinn sat on the floor next to a window, his back against the wall of the empty second-story room, and held his cell phone to his ear.

"You were right to hide out there for the rest of the day." Will's voice was tense. "It wouldn't have looked good to the police for you to be caught leaving a battle scene like that with a 9mm and a sniper rifle in your possession. Is anyone still around?"

Quinn turned and looked out the window, then sat back against the bare wall.

"No, everyone is gone. The street was a freaking mess all day, though. Police, crime scene investigators, and people from the coroner's office swarming around, plus the ambulances and tow trucks. They worked quickly. Probably pressure from the local residents to get this out of the way. What have you found out?"

"Well, we know that was one badass machine gun Marco has. Called the fastest gun in the world. Damn thing shoots two, three thousand rounds per minute. It doesn't so much shoot the enemy as shred them."

"I can attest to that. What in the hell is a civilian like Marco doing with a machine gun like that?"

"Believe it or not, he has a permit for the damn thing." Will sounded intrigued. "According to Marco's permit application, corporate spying in the pharmaceuticals industry is even worse in the United States than in Italy, and the competition won't think twice about hiring gunmen to steal corporate secrets. Says there have been several attempts on his life and several attempted kidnappings and murders at his factory in Italy. The bulletproof glass, the super-thick armor plating, the weapons— his story is that this is all self-defense."

"Did they search the convoy vehicles?"

"Yup. It all checks out with his story. The middle vehicle, that assault vehicle with the machine gun, had vials of medicine stored inside. Medicine, that's all, nothing else. Samples of some new, top-secret heart medication from Marco's factory. Flown in from Italy on his private jet, again to avoid any attempts at robbery. And the FDA confirmed the medication is pending approval. All the evidence seems to prove that Marco's story is correct."

"What it proves," replied Quinn, "is that Marco is a clever bastard. How is this all playing out with the Laguna police?"

"As you can imagine, they are going nuts. It is rare for Laguna Beach to get one murder per year, let alone a bloody massacre. You saw the policemen picking through the bodies and the thousands of rounds of spent ammo. They interviewed

Marco today at the Palazzo, but apparently got nowhere. Marco is playing the victim through all of this. Turning it all around, asking how the local police could let such a horrible attack happen in a sleepy little beach town."

"And the attackers?"

"All Russian thugs. Some were ex-FSB, some straight-out Russian mafia. With one exception—the guy with the rocket launcher was Viktor Orlov."

"I thought so. I read the dossier on him on the flight from Rome. He was no common criminal. Highly educated, descended from Russian nobility. Made his fortune during the collapse of the Soviet Union. A major player, with considerable resources."

"You'd think a guy like that would already have everything anybody could want." Will sounded curious.

Quinn thought for a moment. "Except for one thing, apparently. And he was willing to die for it."

CHAPTER 15

Newport Shores, California

THICK FOG ROLLED IN, RAIN WAS SURE TO FOLLOW, AND QUINN'S only supply of food was running low.

He reached over and grabbed one of the few remaining pieces of beef jerky out of the bag. He chewed as he watched the twinkling lights of the coastline disappear behind a gray veil.

At the same time it was covering the coast, the murky mist spread inland. The tendrils of fog advancing up Coral Cove Lane seemed vaguely hostile, as if they were some sort of silent invasion, swallowing up the streetlights and chimney tops one by one.

A few tentative drops of rain landed on his head and rolled down the back of his neck. One of his legs was asleep, and his other limbs ached as he shifted his position in the damp sleeping bag.

The tiled rooftop of the vacant mansion seemed even more inhospitable than it had the previous day. The luminous dial of his watch told him it was half past eleven and that he was in for another long night.

He reminded himself again why he had decided to stay. Rather, he reminded himself *of* his decision *to* stay, for there was no good reason why he had not packed up camp after dark and ridden his BMW motorcycle out of Newport Shores and back to the comforts of home.

After the carnage of the day, that would have been the sensible thing to do. Coast in neutral, with his engine and lights off, down well past Coral Cove Lane, then start the engine and make his way over to Pacific Coast Highway. Perhaps a stop at a wayside bistro for some real food and drink, and then be home in plenty of time for a hot shower and his own bed.

Yet here he was.

He picked up his night-vision binoculars and scanned. The streets that had been empty in black and white and gray were now just as empty when tinged with green.

His mind insisted on finding specific reasons for why he had stayed. The delivery convoy, after all, had held samples of medicine, and it all fit in with Marco's narrative. Yet there had to be something else.

And that something else was what?

He didn't know. Yet.

The truth was that he had stayed because his instinct told him the real cargo was still out there. And he was determined to wait it out and see what it was. He put the binoculars down and drank from his bottle of water.

The fog was low in the sky. Above it, the gray and white clouds were thinner and spaced out, leaving gaps with glimpses of the heavenly bodies. Stars twinkled here and there. The crescent moon emerged from behind a cloud, adding a silver and white luminescence to its section of the sky.

He was reaching for his binoculars when a black shape glided across the moon.

His hand stayed in midair, frozen on its way to the binoculars. Whatever this object was, he didn't want to miss anything by turning his gaze away.

The black shape moved slowly, taking several seconds to cross his field of vision, and disappeared into a cloud.

He brought the binoculars up and scanned left and right and up and down. Nothing.

What had he seen?

His mind was unable to process the data into anything recognizable. It could not have been the most likely explanation, an airplane. No, this object was much too close—not more than a quarter mile away—to be so silent.

Perhaps a bat? Some nocturnal bird? But there had been no birdlike movement—no flapping of wings, no dive or climb. It had moved almost linearly, from right to left, and much too slowly to be any type of bird or bat.

Moreover, its shape was unlike that of any flying creature. The shape had been oval, or more accurately, teardrop-shaped, like a whale or large fish.

Yet it hadn't undulated, as all fish do. Regardless, no marine creature is capable of leaping in front of the moon.

The crescent moon was once more behind the drifting clouds, and the sky returned to its dull gray. Whatever this black shape was, it was also hiding behind a cloud. Quinn scanned the sky, waiting for the black shape to reemerge, hoping for moonlight that might again illuminate the flying object.

After a long five minutes, a patch of sky brightened, and the moon again moved into clear view. Quinn increased the magnification of his binoculars and searched. Whatever it was, the flying object could not have gone far.

Through the green hue of the binoculars, there was a glimmer of something that was black and round and reflecting the transitory moonlight. That something was low in the sky, emerging from behind a gray cloud hanging over the beginning of Coral Cove Lane.

And that something was moving in his direction.

The fickle moon faded into the next cloud, but he didn't need the moon anymore. The image intensifier in his night-vision binoculars had the capability to take an image in extreme low-light situations and transform it, by an order of magnitude, into a green-tinged but visible replication. As soon as he found the low-flying object, he adjusted his binoculars and zoomed in on his quarry.

It was now on the other side of Coral Cove Lane and moving up the street, just a few feet above the brick chimneys and tiled rooftops of the grand houses. Quinn guessed its speed to be about three or four miles per hour, about the walking speed of a human. From his angle, all he could see was an oval shape, slightly blurry at the edges, a distortion inherent in night-vision technology.

Whether from a gust of wind or deliberate movement, the ghostly object turned to the side for a few seconds, its front turning to the left.

His jaw clenched in recognition.

A *blimp.*

A freaking *blimp.*

A miniature one, to be sure. Not more than fifteen or twenty feet long. But it was all there. The whale-shaped envelope full, no doubt, of helium. The four fins in back. With his binoculars, he glimpsed the whirring propellers below the fins.

And below the envelope, where ordinary blimps would have

a gondola designed to carry humans, was what looked like a large, rectangular suitcase.

Easily large enough to carry, say, a painting.

A shiver ran down Quinn's back, chilling him despite his sleeping bag.

Marco was one clever bastard. He had recognized that any delivery by a conventional vehicle—whether an armored truck or a limousine or the trunk of a battered compact—would inherently impose risk. No matter what precautions were taken, there remained risk that the roads would be sealed off, the vehicle intercepted, the treasure stolen.

So pick something that can fly, but below any radar. Remotely operated. Something that, unlike a drone, makes virtually no noise. The propellers were probably battery driven. No noisy engine, no heat to show up on a thermal imaging camera.

The blimp made its way up Coral Cove Lane. A light rain began to fall, the drops showing as tiny green blurs through his binoculars. The blimp stayed just above the rooftops, like a Peter Pan sailing above the rooftops of London, but without a Wendy, and with the children staying asleep and unaware in the houses below.

Quinn smiled grimly at the attention to detail. By staying above the rooftops, and keeping away from the streets, the blimp further reduced any chance of being seen. It would be difficult for a resident to see, at night and with tree-lined streets, something that was directly over their rooftop. Add into the mix a night shrouded in heavy fog, with a crescent moon and the possibility of rain, and the poor visibility would make it next to impossible to see.

He reflected on the daylight convoy that had been delivering medicine. A decoy, of course, designed to draw in and then massacre any attacker at just the right time, before the real delivery. A crowning touch from Marco.

The rain continued, light but steady, soaking his hair and the outer layer of his sleeping bag. Quinn ignored it and refocused the binoculars.

The airship moved closer. Blurry green raindrops scattered off the top of the blimp and a blurry green mist hung behind the whirring propellers. Floating over gabled rooftops, past carved brick chimneys, its cargo was near the end of a journey that had begun halfway around the world.

The blimp left the cover of the houses along the street and sailed alongside the stretch of private road, over the dark treetops of the forest. Against the foggy black night, it looked like a ghost ship, a ghost ship traveling so silently that it did not even disturb the cloak of fog surrounding it, much less disturb the birds sleeping in the trees or the forest animals curled up in their dens.

The ghost ship sailed past the tops of willow and eucalyptus trees, coming closer and closer, but still out of reach. Quinn clenched the binoculars as the ghost ship entered the grounds of the Palazzo. It sailed over the rows of coiled razor wire hidden in the cypress trees, over the gate and driveway, over the surveillance cameras that covered every inch of the property. All lights on the buildings and grounds were off, as if no one was home.

The ship floated up toward the main entrance to the Palazzo, then veered left over the mermaid fountain. As Quinn had expected, the ship was headed toward the top of one of the turrets.

He scanned the top of the nearest turret with his binoculars. Four green, human shapes emerged on the turret, each holding a green rope. The men stood in a circle, waiting.

The ship hovered above the center of the turret, then

lowered. When it came within reach, the men threaded the ropes through steel rings attached to the bottom of the envelope, stringing the ropes through several different ways before tying them to the turret. When the last knot had been tied, the tethers tested, the men stepped back and waited.

The ghost ship had landed.

CHAPTER 16

Cresta del Mar, California

ON A WARM AND SUNNY DAY, A MOTORCYCLE RIDE UP THE California coast can be exhilarating. On a cool and rainy night, when the wind cuts like a knife through clothes that are soaked through to the skin, it is better classified as an ordeal.

When he parked his bike in his garage, Quinn had to pry his hands from the grips as if they had been frozen on. He strode directly from the garage to his master bath, where, still shivering, he stripped off his clothes, left them in a heap on the tile floor, and turned on the shower just short of scalding.

Minutes later the blessed hot water and bar of soap washed away two days of grime and sweat. After drying off and putting on a clean T-shirt and faded blue jeans, he settled into the desk chair of his upstairs study with a ham sandwich on rye and a cold Negra Modelo beer.

His cell phone, lying on his desk, caught his eye. He was looking forward to the response to the lengthy encrypted text he had sent from the rooftop of the vacant mansion just before he had packed and left for home.

Outside his window, the gray-black rain clouds gathered along the coast were starting to clear. A few stars broke through.

He treasured his status as an independent contractor. It allowed him to serve his country, while still keeping a considerable amount of personal autonomy. And if it brought him the more off-the-wall cases? All the better. He thrived on challenge.

And now he was on the verge of breaking this case.

If the contraband inside that blimp were indeed this valuable painting, then it could be the key. The key that would not only nail Marco for killing Blackwell, but bring down Marco's entire criminal operation as well.

He looked at his watch. A little after two o'clock. Will was still back east, and it would be after five there. He probably wouldn't hear back until tomorrow.

The fatigue of his long stakeout set in. He finished the beer, leaned back in his chair, and closed his eyes. Scenes of the war-zone carnage from the day before floated by in his mind, followed by images of the ghost ship sailing through the night over rooftops and treetops. One was like a nightmare, the other a dream.

At the meeting in the Director's office, Quinn had been skeptical of Professor Hale's narrative of art history. The intense struggle to possess precious artworks had seemed implausible. Men would risk their fortunes, their lives, for strokes of paint on a piece of canvas?

Now, after what he had seen, it was quite believable. The history of art was the history of mankind itself. The good and the bad.

The soft vibration of his cell phone rattled on his desk, and he opened his eyes to see the blue screen flashing the encryption code. It was a phone call, not a text.

"Will, when do you sleep?"

"Not when duty calls, Michael. I just spoke with the Director. Big news, and it relates to your blimp-flying guy."

"Go ahead." Quinn sat up, fully awake.

"That sample of white powder you took from Marco's factory in Calabria? Well, the lab results are in from both the FBI and DEA. Pure, one hundred percent Snow White. No question."

"Damn! I knew it. So the medicine sample in his convoy, his pharma company …?"

"All exist, but as a front for his real operation. Gold star time for you tonight, Michael, with a happy face."

Quinn was already thinking ahead to the fence around the Calabria factory and the state-of-the-art security at the Palazzo. "There's some work to be done."

"And not very much time." Will's voice had a note of urgency. "According to the DEA, the drug has spread like wildfire down the East Coast. It is now deep in Georgia, the Carolinas, and Virginia, in addition to New York and New Jersey. The big city gangs from Harlem to Newark are all fighting over who gets to deal it."

"That's almost the entire East Coast. All in a few months?"

"I'm not done. It looks like Marco is starting his nationwide rollout. That freighter they were loading with the stuff in Calabria? It's headed for Mexico, to a West Coast port called Pueblo Lorito. It so happens that this port is completely controlled by the Mexican cartels. Once their mules get that stuff into California, Michael, the DEA says there will be no stopping it from spreading across the country."

"So what can the DEA do against Marco?"

"That's just it. Marco has them walking into walls. He uses

the Societa without leaving a trace. His plant in Italy is in an area completely run by the mob. All local law enforcement is under their control, and rumor has it that the mob's tentacles spread up into the national government. In other words, both the Italian and Mexican governments are useless. And none of the dealers in the United States will know much, if anything, about Marco. Even if the DEA nabbed some small-time dealer, he would rather die than talk, and it would waste a year. The way this stuff is spreading, they don't have a year."

"And the FBI?"

"Marco launders his money perfectly. As far as the FBI can tell, he is a law-abiding foreign national who pays his taxes and wants to become a citizen."

"He doesn't leave any fingerprints anywhere, does he?"

"Exactly. The DEA desperately wants to stop this stuff before it spreads nationwide. To accomplish that we need to go beyond anything traditional law enforcement can do."

Quinn waited. He knew what was coming.

"That's why," Will continued, "the Director instructed me to inform you that your official mission now is to neutralize and destroy Marco's drug operation, as soon as possible. If you can do that, and if we can get one of Marco's lieutenants to talk, then we can nail Marco for a dozen other things in addition to Blackwell's murder."

"Understood." Quinn's mind churned.

"As a sidebar, Michael, if you can rescue this painting that seems to have started everything, that's fine. This Professor Hale, the friend of the Director's, seems to think it's a big deal. What you do about all that is your call. We'll help, but it's no longer a concern of ours. Your mission going forward is to take down Marco's drug operation. The sooner the better. Clear?"

"Clear."

"Any ideas, my friend?"

"One or two."

Quinn already knew what he wanted to do. Along with putting Marco's heroin operation out of business, he would recover this painting. This hot babe you couldn't take your eyes off of? He would get his hands on her and take her away. What better way to stick it to Marco?

Quinn leaned back in his chair. The conversation ran on through the night, with calls going back and forth, until the first oyster-pink tinge of dawn broke through the gray clouds along the coast. By the time it wrapped up, Will's voice was gravelly and tired.

"Michael," he said before signing off, "I just hope the water's warm."

CHAPTER 17

Pueblo Lorito, Baja California, Mexico

BELOW A GATHERING OF LOW CLOUDS, THE SHADOWY BLACK SHAPE of the Zodiac boat made its way along the outside edge of the cove, keeping as close as possible to the steep rocky boundary.

The black rubber boat slowed as it came up to the seaward tip of the perimeter, then stopped when it reached the point where Quinn could see the lights of the horseshoe-shaped cove.

"This is probably as far as we should go, sir," whispered Petty Officer Danny Jensen, his coxswain. "That moon could come out from behind the clouds any time it wants. We don't want to take any chance of being seen. It'll be a bit longer dive than planned."

"No problem. After five days of dive training, I could swim from here back to Coronado." Quinn checked the zipper on the back of his wetsuit and swung his legs over the side of the Zodiac. He spat in his face mask, rubbed the lens, and pulled the mask over his head. "I would appreciate you being here when I return, though, Jensen."

"Heard and understood, sir."

Quinn slipped off the side of the boat and into the sea. Liquid darkness surrounded him, and the only sound was that of his own breathing. He kicked a couple of times, breathed through his rebreather mouthpiece, and checked his gauges. All was in order. The Draeger rig would be fine for a shallow dive like this, and wouldn't leave any telltale wake of bubbles. He kicked up and gave Jensen the *OK* sign, then sank below the surface again.

The weight of the limpet mine strapped to his chest carried him down faster than he wanted. He adjusted his BCD to slow his descent, and when he was about twenty feet below the surface, he fine-tuned it until he achieved neutral buoyancy. He checked his gear again. On a strap around his thigh was his knife, its serrated steel blade tucked inside its sheath. On one side of a belt around his waist was his flashlight, and on the other side was what Jensen had called the "nail-shooter." He checked his depth and pressure gauges, then the settings on his wrist compass.

With the moon hidden behind clouds, the water surrounding him was as dark as coal. To avoid the risk of using a flashlight, he would have to rely on instruments to keep his bearings. He looked at his dive computer and confirmed the settings and estimated distance to reach the target.

Time to go. He tilted forward until his body was horizontal and began a steady, rhythmic kick toward the sleeping village of Pueblo Lorito.

His breathing through the rebreather mouthpiece was relaxed and controlled, his arms were at his sides, and the power generated by his long dive fins made his forward movement seem effortless. Soon he was in the zone shared by all skilled divers, that zone of equanimity brought about when the quiet liquid world shuts out the chaos and noise of the

112

terrestrial world. In part the escape from gravity and in part the solitude, it was a unique kind of inner peace.

He glanced down at the powerful explosives strapped to his chest and ran though the mission again. In theory at least, it was straightforward. He would need to surface at least once, when he was close enough to visually confirm the target. Then it was a matter of attaching the mine, setting the timer, and heading back to the boat.

The water around him remained inky-black. Shapes moved in the murk—obscure, undulating shapes—curious marine life, but impossible to discern. Quinn cleared away the cobwebs of apprehension and put his mind back in the zone, looking straight ahead and concentrating on his mission.

Six hundred yards, five hundred, four hundred. He was making good progress. The screen on his dive computer blinked that he was three hundred yards from the target.

He kicked his way up until his face mask broke the surface. The full moon behind him was emerging from the clouds, offering improved visibility. He scanned the U-shaped coastline in front of him.

To the right, in a small marina, humble fishing boats rested in their berths, along with a few sailboats.

To the left and in the middle of the coastline were two long piers. The pier on the left was bare, and the pier in the middle was loaded with twenty-foot containers. The berths next to both piers were empty. His attention went to the containers on the middle pier.

The satellite photos had shown the target containers were labeled with the name Pes-Ex, a Mexican seafood company that existed only in cyberspace. In reality, the containers held Marco's massive shipment of Snow White.

Quinn had been concerned that, if the bay were fogged in, he would have to risk surfacing right at the pier to confirm the target. The full moon emerging from behind the clouds, and the fact that the piers were lit up like a car lot, made the concern a non-issue. On the side of each container, Pes-Ex was painted in giant black letters against a stark white background. Target confirmed.

It seemed strange that the piers were deserted, without a single security guard. A closer look showed that not only were the piers deserted, but so was the town's short main street— and, for that matter, what could be seen of the few dark buildings that comprised the small downtown as well.

At the base of the steep hillside across the narrow street from the harbor were four separate guardhouses, spaced well apart along the hillside so that altogether, they could look down on every inch of the main street and marina. He could see the silhouettes of the guards and their rifles inside the lit guardhouses, standing at sentry.

Now the empty streets made sense. The locals knew to stay away from the areas controlled by the *narcotraficantes*.

He ducked his head under the water and floated for a moment. His face had been above water for about thirty seconds. With the light chop of the sea, it was unlikely for anyone to have seen him. He kicked back down to a depth of twenty feet and proceeded forward.

Soon he could make out the front pilings of the pier. The concrete pillars were encrusted with seaweed and barnacles. A few kicks more, and he was underneath the pier. Aware of how lit the topside was, he descended deeper and then kicked forward until he was at the approximate midway point of the pier's underside.

Now would come the tricky part. His mind ran through the training he and Jensen had done. He kicked up until he could feel the wood bottom of the pier, a good five feet below the surface. Running his gloved hands along the old wood, he searched for a suitably smooth area to tether the mine. Pieces of floating debris knocked into him as his fingers felt eyebolts and protruding nail heads.

A few feet back from the center, he found a smooth patch. He brought his flashlight up from his waist and, risking a second of light, obtained visual confirmation. Kicking to stay in place, he put the flashlight back and un-tethered the gray metal limpet mine from his chest.

Holding the helmet-shaped mine with both hands, he brought it up until it was flush against the wood underside of the pier.

The loss of the mine's weight caused his body to float up against the wood. Keeping the mine in place with one hand, he adjusted his BCD with the other until he had achieved neutral buoyancy and was once again vertical. Then he reached down to his belt and brought up the nail shooter.

About the size of a cordless drill, the nail shooter was a self-contained, battery-operated nail gun. He placed the tip of the nail shooter inside one of the four holes around the outside of the mine. When the tip was against the wood he twisted, then compressed the black knob on top. The gun gave a slight jolt as the gas in the combustion chamber ignited and drove the piston down, driving the nail into the wood. He breathed a sigh of relief and moved the tip of the nail shooter over to the next hole.

Five minutes later the mine was secured to the underside of the wood pier. He strapped the empty nail shooter back on his belt and pulled on the mine from all sides. No tide or current would be able to undo his work.

With the tension of his labor, he was sweating inside his wetsuit. He slid back the cover to reveal the programmable timer. When he pressed the buttons he was relieved to see the LED screen light up, the black letters showing the correct time against the blue screen. He looked at his watch, then pressed the buttons to activate and program the timer. He re-checked his watch, then the timer setting. Satisfied, he slid the cover shut, turned away from the mine, and kicked under the pier and back out to sea.

Without the weight of the mine, he was able to set a faster speed for the return trip. There, to his right, were the rocks that meant he was near the tip of the cove. He kicked on, maneuvering around the jagged rocks.

Ahead of him he could make out the solid black patch that was the bottom of the Zodiac. It was waiting a short distance from where it had dropped him off. Quinn breathed a sigh into his mouthpiece, kicked the last dozen yards to the side of the boat, and surfaced.

Jensen, standing in the boat, grinned when he saw Quinn's thumbs-up sign. He glanced at his watch.

"Ahead of schedule, sir. Let's get you back. I understand you have a busy day tomorrow."

CHAPTER 18

Newport Shores, California

A UNIFORMED VALET OPENED THE PASSENGER DOOR, AND QUINN stepped out of the limousine and into a different world from the murky sea of the previous evening.

The circular cobblestone driveway at the entrance to the Palazzo held a double row of luxury cars dropping off the arriving guests. The pleasant chatter of greetings floated through the air, mingling with the bustle of the valets. Drivers maneuvered white Bentleys and black Rolls Royce Phantoms around the verdigris mermaid statues that bordered the marble fountain.

Quinn retrieved his solitary suitcase from the limo, refused the offer of the valet to have the suitcase delivered to his room, and followed the liveried butler through the great double doors and into the foyer. From there a gray-uniformed maid took over, escorting him down the main hallway, through a connecting hallway, over to the guest wing, and upstairs to his room on the second floor. As the door closed behind him, Quinn laid his suitcase on the king-size bed and strode out onto the small balcony.

The balcony had a sweeping view of the rear grounds and the sea beyond. The sun, just beginning to set, was a golden globe touching the horizon. A cluster of dark gray clouds to the north hinted at a possible summer storm. The lawn and pool area below him twinkled with party lights.

He looked around at the property and oriented himself. To his right stretched the lap pool where Sienna had been swimming. Below him, at the outdoor bar and table area where he had been served lunch, groups of party guests mingled. To the left was the free-form pool, which now held floating candles. Most of the large lawn was a carpet of twinkling purple and pink lights. Soft harp music floated up from the rear grounds.

And there, to his far left, was the mansion's other wing: the first floor, which housed the garage containing Marco's car collection, and the second floor, which housed Marco's private gallery.

Somewhere inside that gallery, was there a treasure that had arrived by ghost ship in the dead of night?

In his coat pocket was the note that had come with the formal invitation to, as the flowery script stated, the Annual Midsummer Night's Dream Gala. He dug it out and looked at it again. "Arrangements have been made," the note stated, for Quinn to stay overnight as a guest and to meet with Mr. Leone at 11:00 a.m. sharp the following day for a "private business meeting." No doubt for Marco to show off what he wanted in his private gallery and then to discuss "business."

Even through the flowery script and engraved stationery of the note, the command was palpable. The meeting was not an invitation or even a request. By its wording it was an order, the ruler summoning one of his subjects.

Quinn put the flash of resentment out of his mind. There was much to do. He turned and walked inside.

He lifted his suitcase and checked the settings on the digital lock. If anyone tried to open the lock, an alarm would go right to his cell phone. He slid the suitcase under the bed. After inspecting the well-appointed bathroom, he splashed cold water on his face and glanced at his reflection in the mirror. In his white summer tuxedo coat, black slacks, and black bow tie, he looked the part of the well-to-do party guest.

The memory of the putting-green lawn and the sunny day by the pool was in his mind as he went through the double doors leading to the rear grounds. As he stepped outside into the twilight, he stopped.

Before him lay a forest out of some ancient myth.

Trees were everywhere, white birch and weeping willow and live oak trees, about twelve to twenty foot tall, slender trunks with multiple branches. Canopied by clusters of Spanish moss, their branches almost touching, the trees formed a dense woods intertwined with paths that twisted and turned in every direction. Gray mist floated between the trees, thin in some spots and thick as a Scottish moor in others. And everywhere, floating among the treetops and mist, were constellations of twinkling lights.

The countless tiny lights were the purple and white and pink he had seen from his balcony. Now, inside the forest, from some creator's fine touch in designing their own sky, the colors diffused in subdued variations. The white lights glowed in shades of pearl and seashell, the purple lights in plum and orchid, the pink in cherry blossom and coral. Their combined incandescence glimmered as if it were the twilight of another world.

He stepped into the beckoning forest—for surely that was expected of the visitor—and picked his way along one of the winding paths. His footsteps made a soft crunching noise. He was treading on a forest floor of leaves and bark.

Bits of Spanish moss touched his face and hair as he made his way through the path. Where the mist was heavy, drops of dew clustered on the low-hanging branches that brushed against his coat. The only sound was the crunching of his footsteps. Here and there were whispers, and once he glimpsed a shadowy shape behind a tree, the outline of a couple embracing. But when he stopped to look, no one was there.

After a couple of minutes along the twisting pathways, he stopped and realized with amusement that he didn't know where he was or which direction he had come from.

Behind him came a new sound, the faint sound of someone's breath.

"Would you care for a drink?" asked a gentle female voice.

He turned around to see a young woman carrying a tray with glasses of white wine. The woman was petite, not more than five foot one, with delicate features and milk-white skin. She wore some sort of peasant costume. Trying not to stare, Quinn's gaze went from her face, which was painted in purple and silver, to her ears, which curved up into elfin tips.

The woman took a step back. "Sorry if I startled you. Looks as if this might be your first time here."

"You guessed right. And yes, a drink sounds great." Quinn lifted a glass off the wood tray and gave the girl a reassuring smile. "This is wild. Amazing how they brought all these trees and lights in. They certainly do a party well here."

The wine tasted of honey and clove and other spices. Mead. As he took a second sip, he noticed how the girl was in costume.

Her hair was a proliferation of colored braids, hanging down to her waist in streams of light green and reddish brown. She wore a tiara made of leaves and flowers, and had an eye mask painted on her face, with intricate patterns of silver dots against a purple background. Her loosely-laced leather bodice revealed the upper half of a soft white bosom. A thin lace skirt almost touched the ground, with only the toes of her sandaled feet poking through.

"Yes, 'The Midsummer Night's Dream' is a very special night." She seemed relieved at Quinn's friendliness. Her eyes took on a mischievous look. "There's more you probably don't know about."

"Well, I'd certainly like to learn." Quinn stepped forward and extended his hand. "I'm Michael."

"Heather." She took his hand. Her grip felt weightless. "And, if you are wondering *what* I am—"

"I was."

"I'm a dryad."

"Okay. And a dryad is …?"

"We're tree nymphs. Sort of forest people. We're shy creatures and tend to keep to ourselves. But, once we know you, we can be quite passionate."

"That's certainly good to know, Heather. And are there others like you?"

"Yes, but only here in the forest. You might catch a glimpse of them between the trees. Later on in the evening, outside the forest, some maenads might approach you. *They* aren't shy at all. If this is your first time, watch out for them, they're pretty crazy."

"I'll be most careful. I should probably know better than to drink wine with a pretty dryad in a strange forest to begin with."

"You're safe here." She giggled. "It's out there that things are wild."

"Hm. Now you've done it, Heather," Quinn teased. "You've piqued my curiosity. I'm going to walk through the rest of this forest and see what's there. Maybe I'll see you later?"

"Maybe you will."

She stepped closer and ran her fingers along the lapel of his tuxedo coat. Then, without warning, she put her arm around his neck and pulled his head down toward hers. Balancing the tray of drinks with the other hand, she stood up on her tiptoes, leaned forward, and whispered into his ear.

"I'll be here all night."

A whiff of a fragrance that smelled like rain and musk, and a surprise peck on his cheek, then she was gone, disappearing into the forest.

For a moment, Quinn stood still, savoring the unexpected kiss. He wouldn't mind seeing this Heather again. Holding his glass of mead, he stepped forward on the winding path and made his way through the rest of the night-darkened forest.

A few more turns, and the woods began to thin. The mist dissipated. Stepping around a large weeping willow, he could make out a patch of white luminescence. Moonlight. He was approaching the end of the forest.

The purple-and-pink twilight faded behind him, and the moonlight in front became the dominant light. Ahead was the faint murmur of voices.

Around a curve, he came to the last line of trees. He glimpsed a whitish moon, a starry sky, and the silhouettes of human shapes. The murmuring became louder.

He followed the winding path around a tree dripping with Spanish moss and stepped out from the forest into a clearing. A large, oval-shaped, grassy area stretched to the bluff overlooking the sea. For a moment he stood at the edge of the forest, orienting himself to the panorama before him.

It was the back section of the yard, where visitors ended up after making their way through the forest. The guests stood in groups and couples across the wide lawn, chatting and laughing. Most of them were dressed in summer white, although some of the women wore pastel party dresses. Music floated through the night air, a soft sound of strings being gently plucked.

At the far end of the lawn sat a young woman in a white toga, her long hair a cascade of golden tresses. She was playing a silver harp that she held between her bare legs. Around her on the lawn was a circle of candles. Beyond her lay the aquamarine shimmer of the free-form pool, accented as well with floating candles.

Wandering among the guests, Quinn made his way across the lawn toward the bluff. To his right the lawn ended and the patio began. A large, roped-off area bordered most of the patio. He stopped and sipped his mead as he checked it out.

At one end of the roped-off section was a huge fire pit, at least twenty feet in diameter, built out of stones. At the other end of the section was a large throne, carved out of dark wood. The throne was empty, and the fire pit dark.

The evening's entertainment?

He walked on past the roped-off area and over to a quiet spot at the edge of the bluff where a wrought-iron fence kept visitors from going over the cliff. Beyond the fence, the black sea and starry nighttime sky lay in front of him. A breeze blew in from the dark clouds gathering to the north. He sipped his mead and thought about the coils of barbed wire that surrounded every part of the property that wasn't a sheer bluff.

Behind him someone cleared his throat.

"Well, well, well. Who do we have here?" inquired a sarcastic voice. "And surely, on a night like this, not so pathetic as to be all alone?"

Quinn turned around. He already knew the owner of the irritating, overbearing voice. Sure enough, standing in front of him with his arms folded, flanked by an entourage of women, was Marco.

CHAPTER 19

Calabria, Italy

DEEP IN THE MOUNTAINS OF SOUTHERN ITALY, AMID A THICK forest of fir and pine trees, something disturbed the flocks of sparrows that called the trees home.

It was a sound. A sound the birds did not recognize, and therefore feared.

This late at night, the only sound that should be heard, other than the chirping of the sparrows themselves, was the whistling of the wind blowing in from the nearby Ionian Sea or perhaps the occasional hoot of an owl. But this sound was unfamiliar. A faint, steady buzzing noise sliced through the night air and awakened the sparrows.

On a strip of bare ground below the treetops, strange lights blinked on. These lights were as unfamiliar to the sparrows as the noise.

Alarmed by the intrusion, a chorus of chirping came from the sparrows.

The strange buzzing noise grew louder. Now the entire

roosting aggregation was awake, chirping, heads tilting and eyes glancing around, trying to determine the nature of the sound.

Suddenly, the loud noise was on top of them, and a strange, large object swooped overhead. Sensing immediate danger, the entire flock of sparrows burst out of the trees and circled in the air.

Above the circling birds, the Predator drone climbed up into the nighttime sky. The thirty-foot fuselage glinted in the moonlight, and the steady noise of the engine echoed in the surrounding hills. On the ground, the runway lights began to wink off, and in seconds the hidden airstrip was plunged back into darkness.

Soaring above the treetops, the Predator tilted its wings and executed a wide turn away from the mountains. Arcing across the starlit sky, the craft descended to its cruising altitude and leveled out for its flight.

CHAPTER 20

Newport Shores, California

THE WHITE TEETH FLASHED IN A BRIEF SMILE, THEN THE UPPER LIP curled in a sneer. Marco tilted his head back, awaiting his guest's reply.

Quinn sensed other eyes watching him. Marco's entourage was two women on each side. The woman on the far right was Sienna. When he glanced at her, she looked away, as if she wished she weren't there.

Something was odd. Marco didn't seem the convivial party host Quinn had expected. The women looked ill at ease. Tension hung in the air.

Ignoring Marco's taunt, Quinn smiled and extended his hand, willing himself into bland party guest mode. "Good evening, Marco. Fantastic party you put on here. Thanks again for inviting me."

The man's grip was sweaty, almost greasy, and when the handshake was done, Quinn had to resist the urge to wipe his hand on his pants leg.

Marco's face was flushed, with beads of sweat clinging to the cheeks and to the forehead just below the hairline. His eyes were bright, the pupils like pinpoints.

The man was dusted with his own Snow White. With a strong dose of alcohol surely added in to the mix. And on what better night?

A glint of brass caught Quinn's eye. The grip and pommel of a sword protruded from a brass scabbard hanging around Marco's waist. The solid look of the hilt told Quinn that the sword wasn't a costume piece.

Marco was dressed for the evening in a purple cloak that hung almost to the ground. The velvet cloak had a Napoleonic collar with gemstones sewn along the borders. A bejeweled brooch fastened the cloak around his neck, leaving the cloak open at the chest, revealing the sword.

Open, so as not to interfere with the sword's cutting and thrusting strokes?

Underneath the cloak Marco wore a form-fitting black tunic and leggings. Rings on every finger and heavy gold chain bracelets completed the royal bling.

Marco took a step toward Quinn, spreading his hands apart.

"Yes, my friend, it is indeed a fantastic evening. And that makes what I see all the more pitiful. How can you come to an evening like this, when we celebrate the wonderful pleasures of life, without a date? Do you not have a woman of your own? Look at what you are missing!"

As he looked at the women, Quinn realized this was the original entourage Marco had at the Montage. The three voluptuous, raven-haired women were back, made up like Vegas showgirls, with the raccoon eyes of too much black eye shadow and bronzer that resembled paint. As a concession to the occasion, the women wore medieval-themed polyester gowns that looked as though they came from a costume rental shop.

Sienna, as she had at the Montage, stood apart, standing a few feet away from the others. Her side-swept hair cascaded down over her bare right shoulder, with some sort of sea flower, its petals shaped like a starfish, gracing her exposed, delicate-looking left ear.

Bare-shouldered and sleeveless, the top of her dress was comprised of white pearl-like beads. Tentacles of the shimmering beads trailed up, just over the cup of her breasts, and down, past her hips and, halfway down her upper thighs, as if some lucky white octopus had attached itself to her torso. Below the white beads, her sea foam-colored skirt fluttered in the breeze.

A harsh burst of Italian brought his eyes back to Marco.

"*Venite, cagna! Come here, bitch.*" Marco spat out the curse word and clapped his hands. He grabbed the raven-haired woman next to him by the back of her dress and shoved her toward Quinn. She stumbled forward, almost tripping on the grass, and stood halfway between Marco and Quinn.

"Here, you poor man, take Kimberly. For tonight you can have one of my own *puttane*. I am tired of the bitch anyway. Ha! You will find her well broken in. I have ridden her long and hard, and I am ready for a new filly for my stable."

The acrid remarks hung in the air. No one spoke.

Kimberly, standing between the two men, tried a halfhearted smile, then looked lost and confused. The other women stared down at the ground. Sienna gazed out to sea, her eyes blazing.

Marco turned to one side and with one arm made a sweeping gesture at the party scene behind him. His voice was hoarse and bitter in the nighttime air.

"Look around you. What do you see, eh? Is it not the same

everywhere? *All* women are whores! They are all *puttane!* We give them jewelry, toys, money. They give us their bodies. It is only a matter of degree, of how much we give them, eh? Am I right? Do I not speak the truth? You *know* I am right. Ha!" His fingers touched the underside of his chin, then flicked out at the crowd.

Marco turned back and glanced at Kimberly, then at Quinn. His deep-set eyes glared, and beads of sweat glistened at the top of his forehead.

"You take this bitch. I insist! She is yours for the entire night. She will do whatever you say. The *puttana* should be good for one more ride before she is put out to pasture, ha! Consider her a gift from me. A token in advance of our business meeting tomorrow."

Kimberly stared down at the ground, her arms at her sides, frozen in humiliation.

It was taking every bit of Quinn's willpower not to cold-cock Marco. Did anyone ever stand up to this clown? In his mind, his right fist had already finished a sharp jab to Marco's jaw, followed by a left hook that would draw blood and knock the bastard flat on his back.

Instead, he took a deep breath and exhaled. He grasped Kimberly's hand and patted it.

"I must decline, Marco." Quinn forced a polite smile. "Turns out I already have a date tonight, with a lovely dryad I met in the forest. So I will wish this fine young lady Kimberly well. I'm sure she can do better."

Marco's eyes narrowed to slits. He wasn't sure whether or not the reply was an insult. He stared at Quinn, and his right hand moved to the pommel of his sword and gripped it.

For a moment no one moved.

Something flashed blue through the white fabric of Quinn's tuxedo breast pocket. He looked down at the flashing screen of his cell phone. He had received a text, and he had neglected to set the phone to vibrate only.

"Excuse me." Removing the phone and holding it in the palm of his hand, he glanced down at the screen.

Your client's offer for the Delacroix "Fille dans le jardin" has been received, read the innocent-looking text message from Global Art.

Good news. This meant that the Predator drone had been launched and was in the air over the mountains of Italy.

"So. Is that a message from a lady looking for a date tonight?"

"No." Quinn put the cell phone back into his inside coat pocket. He looked at Marco. "It was only business."

Marco let out a short, harsh bray of a laugh. He released his grip on his sword and shrugged his shoulders.

"Business on a night like this? *Patetico!* You need to get a life. You will excuse me; the show is about to begin."

Marco turned his back to Quinn and motioned to his entourage to follow. He took a step away, then paused and turned his head, tossing a parting remark over his shoulder.

"There are plenty of fish in the sea tonight, eh? Who knows, Mr. Quinn. Perhaps you will get lucky and find yourself a bottom-feeder."

CHAPTER 21

Calabria, Italy

LIKE AN EAGLE WITH A FIFTY-FOOT WINGSPAN, THE PREDATOR drone flew over the sleeping mountain ranges of southern Italy.

Flying just above the treetops, below the level of any radar system, the unmanned aircraft was a stealth operative, watched over by silent stars.

Behind the aerodynamic nose, a complex system of sensors was at work. A variable-aperture infrared camera scanned the nighttime landscape for any sign of hostile action. Other sensors calculated wind speed, related weather factors, and the size and shape and precise location of any object on the ground. A laser-guided targeting system lay at the ready.

Alone in the sky, the craft flew on through the night, the black forests beneath it rolling by in an endless wave.

An order came down from above, from the satellite data link in space, and alerted the electronic brain. It was time for the final leg of the journey.

The titanium-edged wings of the aircraft banked in a wide turn, and the Predator turned away from the mountain range and headed toward the Italian coast.

CHAPTER 22

Newport Shores, California

QUINN WANDERED AWAY FROM THE NOISE AND CROWDS OF THE party, along the lawn next to the wrought-iron fence overlooking the bluff. He stopped at a solitary spot, looked out at the dark sea, and let the breeze cool his anger. His mind processed the new data it had received about the temperament of Marco, and then filed it away in his mental hard drive, in the "possible weakness" folder, for future use.

His mission, of course, came first. But now he also had a score to settle with this megalomaniac. It was only a matter of how and when.

In the sky, the cluster of dark clouds had spread farther south. Beyond the reach of the clouds, the moon still shone a clear white-gold, defending its starry territory.

A sharp *boom* came from behind him, followed by rousing cheers. He turned around. Bright yellow flames crackled high in the night. A bonfire had been lit in the big stone fire pit in the roped-off area.

The show was about to begin.

He made his way back across the lawn toward the fire pit. As he came closer, he noticed partygoers all around him, couples and groups laughing and talking as they strolled across the lawn. By the time he arrived, the crowd was already several feet deep around the rope line. The air was a heady mix of perfume and alcohol and body heat. Zigzagging his way through the throng, he found an empty spot where the rope line met a stanchion.

The fire pit was ablaze, the flames leaping several feet up into the air. Marco sat in the high-backed throne facing the fire pit, his arms resting on the thick wood arms. The brass sword lay by his side, its sharp blade glinting in the firelight. Beads of perspiration glistened on Marco's brow as he stared at the bonfire.

His entourage of women surrounded him, two sitting at his feet and two standing at his side, leaning on the back of the throne. Sienna stood on his right. Her gaze was fixed on the fire.

Music permeated the night. It was no longer the soft music of harp strings. The harpist had been replaced by a reggae band set up at the edge of the lawn. The band played an infinite-loop instrumental, with a booming syncopated bass and heavy, hypnotic *one-AND-two-AND* drumbeat.

A cheer came from the crowd, and a procession of five women, swaying in time to the music, encircled the fire pit.

The women were all in costume, dressed as if they were attending some sort of high-end Renaissance faire. They wore floor-length, embroidered gowns with long sleeves and high collars. Jewelry sparkled from their ears and wrists and necks: layered necklaces, dangling earrings, glittering rings. Their hair was worn up in elaborate bouffants.

All of the women looked to be in their mid-twenties, and all were pretty, with pouty lips and sultry eyes. With their elegant dress, they could have been royalty, nobility from a bygone Europe of centuries ago. Except for the bare feet that peeked through below the skirts, and for the voluptuous, gym-toned bodies that strained against the concealment of the tight-fitting gowns.

One-AND-two-AND. The reggae music played on, the hypnotic beat pulsating through the crowd.

The women stood in place, swaying with the music. Each woman held a long staff wrapped with ivy and topped with a pine cone. Just how did those figure in the evening's entertainment?

"Thyrsus," said a soft voice behind him.

The friendly voice sounded familiar. He turned around to see Heather, the dryad from the forest.

Still in costume with her face paint and dress, she was now barefoot, and her petite body stood up to Quinn's chest. In each hand she held a wineglass of mead. Her gray eyes looked up at him, and her milk-white bosom protruded from the unlaced top of her leather bodice.

"You were wondering what those poles are called," she said.

"You are a mind reader. I was." Heather stood so close he could smell the rain-musk scent from the kiss in the forest. "And what is a thyrus, thyroid, whatever?"

"Thyrsus," she giggled. "They were staffs carried around by maenads. Those crazy nymphs I told you about?"

"Ah, yes, the maenads. But these women don't look anything like crazy. To the contrary, they look like respectable ladies of society."

"Just you wait, Michael." She held up one of the wineglasses. "Anyway, I saw you from the back of the crowd and thought I'd bring you another glass of mead. Would you like some company to watch the show?"

He did some quick calculations. Heather could provide useful cover. He put a hand on her shoulder and moved to the side, making room for her to stand in front of him.

"Absolutely, Heather, I was hoping I'd see you again. I've been saving you a front-row spot, if you don't mind standing a bit close to me. Come on in."

She squeezed in front of him and handed him his wineglass. Holding her glass in both hands, she leaned back so that her backside pressed against Quinn's body. He looked down at her unruly, slightly damp mop of green and reddish-brown braids leaning against his chest, and at the inviting fair skin of her cleavage.

A crackling sound came from the direction of the fire pit.

The costumed women around the stone pit were holding their staffs out and into the fire. They pulled them back out, and now the pinecone tops of the staffs were flaming torches. The women held them aloft, swaying to and fro with the beat of the music.

A murmur of excitement rippled through the crowd.

One-AND-two-AND. The music pulsed through the nighttime air. The reggae band had kicked the volume up a notch, and several couples in the crowd were swaying to the beat.

Holding on to the flaming torches with one hand, the women reached up behind their necks with their other hands. The high, formal collars of their gowns came off in their hands, as if they had been attached with Velcro.

The women threw the detached collars into the fire. Brief flashes of colored flame, bright green and royal blue, erupted as the pieces of fabric were consumed.

Cheers came from the crowd.

The women reached back again with their free hands, fiddling with their costumes. Suddenly the sleeves and shoulder sections of their gowns came off, and the elaborate hairstyles came undone, the long tresses of blonde and brunette hair cascading down the exposed shoulders.

The women tossed the pieces of fabric into the fire, and a rumble came from the crowd as larger flashes of blue and green flame erupted.

One-AND-two-AND. The music volume kicked up another notch. The drummer pounded the beat home with his snare and bass.

Many in the crowd were swaying to the hypnotic rhythm. Quinn looked down to see Heather swaying as well, her gaze fixed on the dancers. Her mop of green and reddish-brown hair pressed against his chest. With the heat from the fire pit, beads of sweat formed along her shoulders and the top of her bosom. Her arms were at her sides, her right hand holding her wineglass.

He glanced at his watch. This was a good time. He slipped his hand into his right pocket. Putting his left hand on her shoulder, swaying back and forth with her body, he covered the top of her glass with his right hand. Her gaze stayed fixed on the dancers as he dropped the pill into her glass of mead.

The women around the fire pit now wore the equivalent of bare-shouldered, sleeveless, low-cut gowns. Their hair was disheveled, and rivulets of perspiration ran down their necks and backs, glistening in the firelight. Quinn found their transformation from staid Renaissance nobility to wild libertines exciting and wondered how far they would go.

He glanced over to the left of the fire pit. Marco sat in his throne and watched the show with a sneer of satisfaction. Lines of sweat ran down his face, and his dark eyes glittered in the reflected light of the fire. Around him the four women, Sienna included, were all gazing at the show.

Another rumble came from the crowd as the women ripped

off their jewelry and tossed it into the pit. Rings, necklaces, and bracelets traced small glittering arcs through the air, followed by bright flashes of colored flames from the bonfire.

One-AND-two-AND. The beat was relentless, throbbing everywhere.

The women waved their torches in the air and swayed to the rhythm of the music. They reached around with their free hands and tugged at the backs of their dresses. The rumble from the crowd swelled to a roar as what was left of the women's dresses fell away from their bodies, crumpling in little piles at their feet.

The women were now clad only in what looked like loincloths.

In unison, the women scooped up their dresses from the ground and tossed them into the pit. The crowd cheered as large, bright flashes of blue and green flame burst from the bonfire.

One-AND-two-AND. The ground seemed to vibrate with the pulsating bass. The crowd was growing raucous, pressing in on all sides. Quinn wrapped his arms around Heather.

The women held their lit torches with both hands, raising them high over their heads as they swayed with the music. Their bodies, glistening in the firelight and moving with the supple grace of dancers, were a spellbinding sight. Shoulder and back muscles gleamed in definition as the women waved their torches. Firm glutes protruded from the sweat-soaked loincloths, and the abs curved down into taut, slim waists.

One-AND-two-AND. The mesmerizing music wafted over the fire and the dancers and the crowd.

The dancers shimmied their shoulders, rolled their hips, and whipped their torches in sinuous curves. Sweat dripped from skin of molten bronze, rivulets running down necks and backs, beads of perspiration flicking off pendulous breasts that shook and gleamed in the firelight. Their hair hung down in damp disarray, shaking with the movement of the bodies, sticking here and there to wet skin. The women tilted their heads back and closed their eyes, as if in some sort of rapture.

The sheer animal magnetism of the spectacle was overwhelming. A prickling sensation crawled up Quinn's skin, and he noticed goose bumps on his wrists and forearms. His face was flushed, and he was sweating.

One-AND-two-AND. The music worked like a sorcerer's spell.

Feral desire spread like wildfire. Moans and screams came from the crowd. Couples groped each other with passionate abandon, dropping their drinks to the ground.

Heather caressed his arms while she swayed with the music. Sweat ran down her bosom, disappearing into the depths of her half-unlaced leather bodice. A wild urge seized Quinn, to rip open the rest of her bodice and caress a soft white breast. He forced his mind clear, and noted with satisfaction that her wineglass was empty.

A chorus of shrieks brought his attention back to the bonfire.

One of the women whipped her torch overhead in rapid circles. With a final scream, she tossed it into the bonfire. As she let go, the woman spun around in a slow half circle, then appeared to faint, her eyes closing and her body crumpling to the ground. The crowd roared and surged forward against the rope-line, anxious to see what would happen next.

Two of the other dancers leaned their torches against the stone side of the fire pit and bent over to pick up the woman on the ground. One picked her up by her shoulders, the other by her feet. The woman hung limp in their arms, her eyes closed, her perspiration-soaked hair almost touching the ground.

Their dancers' bodies glistened in the firelight as they

swung the woman back and forth. They positioned themselves as though they were going to toss her into the fire. The dancers on the other side of the bonfire stood still, holding their torches and watching.

One-AND-two-AND. The dancers swung the woman's limp, naked body in time with the music.

Quinn had assumed the fainting spell was part of the show. Now he wasn't sure. What the hell were these women going to do with the beautiful naked body they held? The fire pit was at least twenty feet wide and was a raging inferno all the way across. No way they could toss her that far. This wasn't some walking-quickly-across-hot-coals party stunt.

The music stopped.

The noise from the crowd receded to a murmur as everyone watched.

The two dancers continued to swing the naked body of the apparently unconscious dancer side to side, increasing their arc with each swing.

The drummer began a slow drum roll, increasing the volume and tempo each time the naked woman's body reached the top of an arc.

The crowd noise swelled again.

Back and forth, the dancers increased the arc of each swing. The resonating drum roll grew louder and louder. *Ooohs* and *ahhhs* came from the crowd as the body seemed to hang in the air at the top of each swing.

Then shrieks erupted from the crowd, and Quinn's jaw dropped open, as with one mighty swing, the dancers flung the naked woman into the center of the bonfire.

CHAPTER 23

Calabria, Italy

THE EYE OF THE PREDATOR, AN INFRARED CAMERA, LOOKED DOWN as the aircraft made a wide turn in the nighttime sky and circled back for another pass over the target structure.

On the first pass, the images transported up the satellite data link had shown signs of possible human life inside the target structure. These signs were confirmed when the image intensifier had zoomed in for close-ups of the building and the guardhouse. Seconds later an untraceable phone call was made to the cell phones of the guards in the guardhouse. When the surprised guards answered their phones, a computer-generated voice dictated an urgent warning to evacuate, then hung up.

As the Predator made a wide turn over the dark countryside, the infrared eye picked up the sudden flurry of activity from the target structure. Figures streamed out of the building and the guardhouse, piled into the cars and trucks in the parking lot, and raced away from the building. The vehicles sped down the single asphalt road that led to the highway.

Now, as the Predator headed back, the infrared eye focused on a building that was deserted. The evacuees had fled in such haste that all the exit doors to Leone Compagnia were left wide open.

Lights burned inside the guardhouse and building, but no one was there.

These pictures were transported up the satellite data link, and in response a new order was sent to the electronic brain.

A laser beam shot out of the Predator and focused on the center of the building's roof. There the beam stayed, pulsing, sending its signals back up to the aircraft. The brain inside the Predator made the necessary calculations for distance and trajectory. Another order was sent.

Twin white streaks crossed the dark sky as the laser-guided Hellfire missiles shot toward the earth. The Predator watched from above, recording the two small clouds of dust and shattered concrete that erupted as the missiles struck their target.

For a millisecond, the two-story building shook, but it withstood the two entry holes made by the missiles. For that millisecond, it looked as if the reinforced concrete structure would survive the double wound.

Then the cloud of explosive fuel dispersed by the thermobaric warheads inside the building ignited.

A massive, white-hot fireball erupted high into the sky. In an instant, the entire building disintegrated. Every inch of concrete and steel, from the guardhouse in front to the delivery trucks in back, was demolished by the tremendous force of the sustained shock waves.

As quickly as it had appeared, the fireball vanished, leaving behind a giant cloud of gray-white smoke. The smoke surged outward on all sides, obscuring the area where the building had once stood.

Then, as the burning gases cooled and the pressure dropped, the smoke reversed course and withdrew into itself. The churning mass of dust and gas thickened and billowed, and then formed into the classic shape of the mushroom cloud.

The massive cloud floated up into the nighttime sky, higher and higher, until all that was left on the ground was a layer of smoking rubble.

CHAPTER 24

Newport Shores, California

SHE MUST HAVE BEEN A GYMNAST, AND ONE WHOSE SKILLS WERE at Olympic level.

The thought flashed into Quinn's mind as he watched the lithe naked body vault out of the center of the bonfire, twist itself across the treacherous flames, and land on the ground on the opposite side of the fire pit.

The woman landed evenly on both feet. She stood straight, head held high, her face ecstatic in triumph, her arms flung out wide.

The crowd had been stunned into silence when the woman had been thrown into the fire. Now they gave a collective gasp of relief, followed by cheering at the success of the death-defying feat.

If it was a gymnastic-style vault as it appeared, it was beyond extraordinary, as it had been done without the momentum of a runway. Yes, there had been some momentum from being tossed. And, hidden in the middle of the flames, there must have been some sort of vaulting table, raised up so that she could spring off it without burning her hands. Regardless, it was still a hell of a stunt, and this woman was no ordinary dancer.

Then again, no ordinary dancer would be posing naked before her audience after just vaulting through a bonfire, her voluptuous breasts and toned thighs glistening with sweat, her mane of wet hair a disheveled tangle.

As the cheering died down, a loud clanging noise came from the side. Quinn looked over at the source of the noise.

Marco had stood up from his throne, knocking the sword to the floor. He stood with his back to the crowd, talking on his cell phone. His entourage of women had disappeared. Two of Marco's bodyguards stood a few feet away.

The cell phone in Quinn's inside coat pocket vibrated. He removed it and read the text.

Your client's offer for the Delacroix "Fille dans le jardin" has been accepted, read the innocent-looking text from Global Art.

Quinn smiled to himself. The armed Predator drone had done its work. Marco's Snow White heroin factory was no more. He glanced back at the empty throne.

Marco paced back and forth, talking on his cell phone, gesturing with his free hand. His features were contorted in a scowl, and his brow shone with perspiration. He stopped to pick up his sword, then turned and strode away from the fire pit and toward the main house, motioning for his bodyguards to follow.

The band struck up a slow-tempo version of the reggae theme they had been playing. Shrieks of laughter came from the direction of the fire pit.

The shrieks came from the dancers. Several men from the audience had surrounded them. They were pouring their glasses of mead over the naked, sweating bodies of the dancers, and then rubbing the mead in with their hands. The dancers raised their arms in the air and giggled and shrieked as the cold liquid streamed over their shoulders and down their bodies.

Screams and splashing noises came from the pool. Groups of partygoers were falling or leaping into the water. Some of the women had removed their party dresses and were giggling and splashing one another.

Aroused by the bonfire spectacle, the crowd was now in a bacchanalian frenzy. Couples everywhere were kissing and groping each other with abandon. Men were grabbing any woman who looked unattached, pulling down the women's shoulder straps and pouring their glass of mead on the women's hair and shoulders.

Something jostled Quinn's shoulder. Two women squealed as they toppled over, a heavyset man on top, with arms around both of the women. He stepped away from the threesome.

From behind him, arms wrapped around his waist. He turned around, and a damp tousle of green and reddish-brown hair leaned against his chest. Heather was hugging him.

She looked up at Quinn and smiled. Then she let go of him, yawned, and stretched.

"I'm so sleepy," she murmured, her eyes drowsy behind the purple and silver paint. She put her arms back around his waist. "Would you like to come up and see my room?"

"I'd like nothing better." Quinn put his arm around her to protect her from the crowd and guided her forward, using his free arm to navigate.

The crowd around them was now a free-for-all of bodies groping and grabbing and bumping into one another. A burly man poked his arm through the crowd and grabbed a fistful of Heather's braids. Quinn knocked the man's arm away, then landed a quick knife-hand strike to the man's throat. The man made choking noises and fell back into the crowd.

Something tugged at Quinn's free arm. He raised his arm, ready to strike again, when he recognized the familiar feminine voice.

"Michael!"

He brought his arm down and turned his head in the direction of the voice. There, over to the side.

Sienna.

Her eyes were wide with fright. Her sideswept cascade of hair was askew, and sweat ran down her face and neck. Still wearing the bare-shouldered, low-cut gown, she crossed her arms against her chest to protect herself from the jostling crowd.

A red-faced man pushed his way in from the crowd, eyeing Sienna. He reached out and grabbed the top of her dress, just above her breasts.

Quinn lunged forward and shoved his elbow hard into the man's nose. The man screamed and staggered backwards, bright red blood streaming down his face.

"Oh!" Sienna had just noticed the sleepy-eyed Heather in Quinn's other arm. "I didn't—I mean, I—" Her cheeks flushed, and she turned around and ducked her head. Keeping her arms crossed, she zigzagged her way back into the throng of partygoers.

"Wait!" yelled Quinn.

He pushed forward into the crush of partygoers, his free arm flailing, searching the area where Sienna had been standing.

He was too late. She had vanished into the crowd.

CHAPTER 25

Newport Shores, California

IN THE DARK ROOM, QUINN'S WATCH DIAL FLASHED. IT WAS 2:45 a.m. Time to go.

Quinn turned over in the bed and looked at Heather. She lay fast asleep, breathing peacefully, her chest rising and falling under her bedcovers. She had fallen asleep in the hallway, and he'd had to carry her into her room and put her in bed.

He slid out of Heather's bed and crept over to the window. The grounds of the Palazzo were empty and dark, and the sky was a gray-black haze. The storm clouds from the north had moved in during the night and covered most of the sky. He turned away from the window and walked to the door, his mind on what lay ahead.

As he put his hand on the doorknob, he turned for a last look at the sleeping figure. Heather's braided dryad-hair was strewn across the white pillow, and the corners of her lips were turned up in a smile of innocent sleep. She was in a deep slumber and would stay that way for several hours. The sleeping pill he had put in her drink had been a bit stronger than needed, but she would be fine in the morning.

When they had walked through the hallways on the way to Heather's room, Quinn had made sure they were seen, hugging and chatting, by every visible surveillance camera. That surveillance video was meant to be the last any camera would see of him tonight. Now, as he left her room, he flattened himself to the walls and avoided the cameras in the corners.

The hallways were empty, with only a few wall sconces providing dim lighting. His room in the guest wing was three hall turns away from Heather's. In less than two minutes of stealthy movement along the walls, he was inside his room.

His suitcase hadn't been moved. Even if they had x-rayed it, the lead-shielded compartment would have revealed only clothing and toiletries. He placed the suitcase on top of his bed and opened it, then dug down through the clothing to the hidden compartment. Everything was there as he had left it. He stripped off his party clothes.

In a few minutes he was dressed, head to toe, in the black clothing that was non-reflective and also blocked infrared technology, and was thus invisible to night-vision cameras. Next came the body-armor assault vest and his hip holster.

He checked his HK 9mm and tucked it into its holster. From the suitcase, he removed a generic-looking sports watch, various small tools to take with him, and a spare clip for his 9mm, and laid them all on his bed.

One by one, the tools and ammo clip were inspected and inserted into the pouches of his vest. He removed his Patek Philippe dress watch and put on the sports watch. His fingers felt the buttons on the bezel and the recessed button in back. The sports watch was far from generic; its controls would pace his mission and also protect it.

Almost ready. He reached into the suitcase and pulled out the quiver.

The quiver, named because of its resemblance to an archer's case for carrying arrows, was a black steel tube with a shoulder strap and a locking cap at one end. It had been invented a little over three years ago to be used in those special circumstances when operatives needed to transport valuable documents or artworks while keeping both hands free.

Since its inception, it had been used twice. Once, to move some valuable parchment scrolls, written in Aramaic and of ancient origin, out of a troubled country in the Middle East. The second time had been to bring a Japanese picture scroll out of an unfriendly country in Asia. Both times, it had been pointed out, the missions had been successful.

Quinn turned the cold steel tube over in his hands. His fingertips ran along the ridged edges of the locking cap and felt the round bumps at the bottom and top of the tube. He glanced at his watch, then back at the tube as his mind ran through the security features.

The tube's cap, when locked, could only be opened by a signal sent from his watch. The GPS unit inside the tube would, in the event things went wrong, be tracked by his watch. The tube itself was made of metal strong enough to withstand heat up to four thousand degrees Fahrenheit, had an electroshock theft deterrent, and would remain watertight at the bottom of the sea.

It would survive anything that could happen tonight.

"Fail-secure" was the term Will had passed on to him from its creators in the tech department.

Quinn slung the quiver over his shoulder and adjusted the shoulder strap until it was tight and the quiver was snug against his back. He closed and locked the suitcase and placed it back under his bed.

He drew his 9mm twice, to make sure there were no snags. After a pat-down of his vest pockets, he took a last look around his room, opened his door, and stepped out into the empty hallway.

CHAPTER 26

Newport Shores, California

THE ENTRANCE TO THE PRIVATE ART COLLECTION OF THE Palazzo, like that of many wealthy art collectors, was guarded by a state-of-the-art security system. No expense had been spared on a saturation motion-detector system that covered every inch of floor space, a closed-circuit video system that monitored every piece of artwork 24/7, and a massive stainless-steel door, worthy of a bank vault, with steel lock-bars that could only be opened by the biometric information from the owner's right hand.

And, as with most state-of-the art security systems guarding private art collections, little to nothing had been done about the attic above.

Quinn reached up to the ceiling and fingered the padlock that locked the pull-down attic entrance door. As he stood on the back of an upholstered wing-back chair—which together with a pole lamp and a landscape print, decorated the end of the deserted guest-wing hallway—he reminded himself of the reason for this seeming neglect.

It was simple logistics. The paramount concern for most art thieves is to remove as many desired artworks as possible in the least amount of time. Utilizing the attic, rather than a door or window, added dangerous layers of uncertainty and delay, and the thief must still deal with the inevitable motion-detector system.

The layout of the Palazzo made this approach even more challenging. The closest attic entrance was in the ceiling at the end of a guest-wing hallway, on the opposite end of the property from the art gallery.

In spite of this, Quinn had argued to Will, the attic was the most logical point of entry to break into Marco's private art gallery. The attic door provided relatively easy access, and in the guest wing he would already be close to it. Furthermore, he was only after one specific artwork, and, with the given mission parameters, he would have plenty of time to make the long crawl and deal with whatever was in the way. In the end, Will had reluctantly agreed that climbing into the attic was the most viable option.

"Sometimes simple and low-tech is the way to go," Will had said.

Now, as he removed a pair of bolt cutters from a vest pouch while balancing on the back of the wing-back chair, Quinn glanced down at the empty hallway and revisited the wisdom of this decision. Simple and low-tech was not without its risks. A guest-room door down the hall could open, a light-sleeping guest could poke their head out and see an apparent burglar, and Quinn would be in a great deal of trouble.

He wrapped the bolt cutters and padlock in a rag to minimize the noise. With a muffled *snap*, the shackle of the lock gave way to the bolt cutters. He pulled down the square wooden door and heaved himself up and into the attic.

It was, as he expected, hot and stuffy, even on a cool night. Squatting on his haunches, he pulled the entry door back up and closed it. He removed his head lamp from a vest pouch. Tightening the elastic band around his head, where beads of sweat were already beginning to form at his hairline, he set the LED light to flood, turned it on, and examined his surroundings.

To his relief, there were no surprises. It looked like any other attic. He was surrounded by a low-ceilinged morass of ducting, pipes, beams, and drywall. Spider webs proliferated among the rafters, and everything was covered in a layer of dust. The attic had no windows, only the occasional vent. As the Palazzo's main buildings contained plenty of air-conditioned and heated rooms for any needed storage, the attic remained unfinished, without any flooring or electricity. He would have to stay on the wood beams all the way, lest he put his foot down and come crashing through someone's drywall ceiling.

From a vest pouch, he unfolded a copy of the house floor plan and looked at it for the umpteenth time. He practically had it memorized. He folded the paper, put it back in the pouch, and looked around the attic.

"It's likely a cramped mess up there," Will had cautioned as they had reviewed the architectural plans of the Palazzo. "You'll be crawling the length of a damn football field in the dark, with who knows what around you."

Quinn's head lamp shone on the maze of wood beams and rafters in front of him. He crouched down, balancing on the beams on his hands and knees. Moving one hand, then one knee, followed by the other hand and other knee, he crawled forward, ignoring the cobwebs that brushed his forehead. This was indeed going to be a slog.

But it would be a cakewalk compared to other missions. No enemy fire to worry about. On the contrary, the enemy was quite preoccupied.

Hell yes, this was doable. And the prize, the treasure, was waiting for him.

CHAPTER 27

Pueblo Lorito, Mexico

IN THE DEAD OF NIGHT, THE QUIET COVE OF PUEBLO LORITO looked much like it did in the days of old Mexico, when the hardy souls who eked out a living fishing and diving in the waters were asleep in their adobe dwellings.

Sitting alone in his guardhouse at the base of the hillside overlooking the cove, the uniformed Mexican guard yawned and gazed out to sea. The marina was as quiet as a graveyard. The black water of the little bay was as smooth as glass.

Holding his rifle across his lap, the guard reached down and opened the bottom drawer of his old metal desk. It was time for his nightly ritual.

He removed a bottle of tequila and a bottle of Kahlua. After filling his thermos cup half-full with steaming hot coffee, he added a good dose of Kahlua, then filled the cup almost to the top with tequila. Putting his feet up on the desk, he leaned back in his chair.

The white shipping containers marked Pes-Ex were still stacked on the middle pier. The rumors floating among the guards said that this shipment was of great value, and that the trucks from the *narcotraficantes* would be coming soon.

He raised the steaming cup to his lips and smiled as the familiar warmth of the coffee and liquor spread through his insides.

Something didn't seem right.

He scanned the marina. Nothing there that he hadn't seen countless times before.

A rumbling noise sounded somewhere below him. His thermos cup shook. Was this the beginning of an earthquake?

Then a massive *boom* echoed around the cove, rattling his guardhouse to its foundation. He dropped his thermos cup in his lap and jumped up, oblivious to the pain of the spilled hot coffee and to the sound of his rifle clattering to the floor.

The center of the middle pier had erupted in a gigantic plume of ocean water, at least fifty feet high. Lit by the halogen lights of the marina, the plume was a mix of churning black water and streaks of white froth that shone like slices of silver. Tossing around inside the plume, glinting in the lights, were pieces of white metal, pieces that the guard recognized as the remnants of the cargo containers that seconds ago had been sitting on the pier.

For a moment, the massive plume seemed to hang in the air. Then, in giant arcs of water curving outward like jets from a fountain, the plume cascaded back down to the ocean, jagged white chunks of the metal containers and dirty brown fragments of the wooden pier crashing into the sea as if from some sort of meteor shower.

As the guard stood frozen in position, there came another sound—groaning wood and crashing metal. The blast had obliterated the center two-thirds of the pier, and now the two jagged ends, with nothing to support them, collapsed inward. The remaining cargo containers banged into one another as they slid into the churning sea, and the wooden ends of the pier followed them, disintegrating into chunks of floating driftwood and debris.

CHAPTER 28

Newport Shores, California

HE MAY HAVE BEEN INSIDE ONE OF THE MOST OPULENT MANSIONS in California, a few feet away from the caresses of ocean breezes, but Quinn's senses told him he was crawling through some sort of dark, dirty cave.

His knees ached from the sharp-edged beams, and his neck cramped from ducking below rafters. Dust crusted his eyes and nostrils. Sweat dripped off his forehead and plopped onto the wood beams below him. His head lamp shone on truss works of beams and rafters ahead.

Hand, knee, other hand, other knee. His path took him through a never-ending series of spider webs, webs whose gossamer bits tore off and stuck to his face and neck. In the darkness, he felt little stings that may have been insect bites, and off to the sides were strange skittering noises. What were they? Probably spiders angry at his interference, or rats or bats or whatever the hell else lived up here.

What if some of the spider webs he was crawling through

were home to poisonous spiders? What kinds were there? The black widow, of course. And another one, not as well known. Recluse? That was it, the brown recluse spider. It was said that you can't even feel their bite, and yet the deadly venom can spread through the body in minutes.

The attic seemed to go on forever. What if it did? Would he find the bones of those who died from recluse spider bites? The scrawling of ancient attic dwellers?

The vibration of his cell phone was a welcome visit from the outside world.

The painting "Fille dans le jardin" will be available for your inspection tomorrow at 2 p.m., read the text message from Global Art Funding.

The Mexico scuba-dive mission had been successful. The massive shipment of Snow White was now a floating part of the ecosystem of the great Pacific Ocean.

He resumed his crawl.

From the clues he had picked up about Marco's temper, having his drug empire crumble around him in a matter of hours would make the man go ballistic. He might be conducting an emergency phone conference to placate angry contacts in the Societa. Or rushing on his way to a hastily arranged meeting in Italy or Mexico. Regardless, Marco would be preoccupied for the next several hours.

The last thing on Marco's mind tonight would be his art collection.

The attic wall curved. That meant he was over the main section of the house. Somewhere below him was the grand foyer with its circular rotunda, the restaurant-size kitchen, and the elegant living room he had glimpsed on his first visit. All would be quiet now, locked up for the night. Until the break of day, when the kitchen crew and housekeeping staff would arrive to brew fresh coffee and begin the cleanup from the Midsummer Night's Dream party.

Also somewhere below him were the main sleeping quarters, with the master bedroom and the secondary bedrooms.

Sienna would be in one of those rooms. No more than thirty, forty feet away. Was she asleep? Alone?

Above him there was a sound, a tapping noise on the roof.

He froze in place, his senses alert. His heart pounding, he turned off his head lamp.

Tap-tap-tap. It repeated above him, then somewhere over to the side. *Tap-tap-tap-tap.* What the hell?

The tapping noise spread to several sections of the roof at once and got louder. The sound increased in rhythmic waves, in all directions, until it became a steady drumbeat across the entire roof. Quinn held his breath as he listened.

Then his brain recognized the noise, and he exhaled. It was merely rain. A summer rain falling on the tiled roof. He remembered the gathering storm clouds he had seen outside Heather's window.

He turned his light back on and resumed his crawl. The rhythmic drumbeat of the rain was welcome company. It could prove a blessing in disguise, for the noise of the rain could serve as cover for any inadvertent noises he might make.

The attic curved again, and now he was over the other wing of the property, the wing that held the private art gallery.

He scanned the area in front of him for a large HVAC duct that, based on the house plans, would be his point of entry. The vent was wide enough for a human to slip through.

The "propeller heads," as Will referred to the cybersecurity specialists, had come up with an ingenious approach to fool the surveillance system of the gallery. It was simple in concept but sophisticated in execution.

After hacking through the encryption codes of the Palazzo's surveillance systems, they had developed the ability to neutralize the entire motion-detector system while the control room instruments continued to read that the system was on. In addition, they had created a continuous-loop video, showing the always-lit gallery undisturbed in every room, which overrode and blocked out what the cameras saw. The continuous-loop video even showed an exact copy of the surveillance system's digital clock, showing the correct time in the lower right-hand corner of the monitor.

The video surveillance system and motion-detector system were both hardwired to the monitors in the control room of the maintenance building. It was impossible for an intruder to escape detection if the system were working, and thus was critical that the propeller heads' blocking system work.

There it was. Not more than fifteen yards ahead and to the left. The silver, corrugated duct looked clean and reflected in his head lamp.

Time for the next step. The key that would open the gallery. To minimize risk of discovery, the propeller heads were waiting for a text from Quinn before they activated their blocking system.

Would like to view "Fille dans le jardin" at 3 p.m., Quinn texted to Global Art.

Crouched on the wood beams, he waited. A drop of his sweat plopped on the wood beam below him.

His cell phone vibrated in response.

Confirmed. You will be able to view "Fille dans le jardin" at 3 p.m. Repeat, confirmed.

This meant the blocking system had been activated. The guards in the control room would see nothing but a quiet art gallery with a functioning motion-detector system.

The gallery was open.

He crawled up to the duct and removed a knife from his vest pocket. The blade cut easily through the duct material. He lifted the ducting away. The lit showroom was visible through the vent grill. With his screwdriver, he removed the screws from the edges of the grill.

Taking care to avoid any noise, he laid the grill and screws to the side. Next, he removed a coiled rope from a vest pouch. He tied one end to a four-by-six beam and lowered the rest of the rope through the ten-foot-high ceiling until it dangled a foot above the floor. After a glance at the showroom, he removed his head lamp and put it back into its vest pouch.

Show time.

Taking a deep breath and thinking a silent prayer for the expertise of the propeller heads in cybersecurity, Quinn swung his feet and legs through the open vent, grabbed the rope, and lowered himself down toward the polished marble of the gallery floor.

CHAPTER 29

Newport Shores, California

IT WAS A GALLERY UNLIKE ANY HE HAD EVER SEEN.

The room beckoned as if it were a work of art itself. Soft accent lighting, ornate inlays in the marble flooring, and coffered mahogany ceilings invited the visitor to linger and explore.

None of the compromises one would find in a traditional gallery or museum were evident. No drop-ceiling fluorescent lighting, no thick glass covering the paintings, no generic furnishings.

He stood in the main showroom, which looked to be about forty feet long. To his left was the gallery's foyer. The stainless-steel entrance door shone in the light. The foyer was furnished with a three-piece, eighteenth-century salon suite, a settee with two matching armchairs. A seascape hung over the settee, and a small mahogany table held a vase of cut flowers.

His gaze turned back to the main showroom. Clearly, this

gallery was designed for only two classes of visitors: Marco by himself and Marco with an invited guest.

Each artwork hung in its own space, with LED lights recessed into the ceilings, to bring out the full color palette of each work. With careful use of dividers and accessories, each painting drew a visitor toward it as if it were the only exhibit to see. No compromise had been made, no expense spared.

His Vibram rubber soles tread noiselessly on the marble floor as he strode the length of the showroom, glancing at each of the paintings. He kept a respectful distance, for the paintings themselves would each have their own motion sensors separate from the Palazzo's surveillance system.

In his research, he had studied Interpol reports of the world's most valuable stolen artworks, and now he recognized several of them. Van Mieris's *A Cavalier*, Caravaggio's *Nativity*, Rembrandt's beautiful *Storm on the Sea of Galilee*. It was a museum of the missing. The main room of the gallery was a showcase of the world's most-valuable stolen art.

But showed no sign of what he was looking for.

Beyond the showroom lay a hallway, lit with candle-shaped lights tucked into alcoves.

He padded into the inner sanctum. It soon twisted and turned into a labyrinth of short connecting hallways. On one wall in the middle of each short hallway was a paneled mahogany door leading, presumably, to a room.

The architectural plans had shown the foyer and one massive room. The maze of hallways and rooms had been added afterward. All the doors looked the same, paneled mahogany with brass lever handles. No numbers or signs or directory.

Where to start?

He opened the first door and looked into a room containing paintings by seventeenth-century Spanish artists. Portraits of bearded old men stared back at him. The next room showcased works by the English Romantics, with idyllic scenes of young maidens by a pond or in a forest.

Each room was dedicated to a specific genre. That might give a clue as to their order.

The next door opened to a room displaying ancient Egyptian artifacts, sculptures of terra-cotta and stone. Then came a room full of detailed Chinese porcelains, colored in blue and red and black.

Clouds of concern gathered in Quinn's mind. There seemed to be no particular order in the way the gallery beyond the main showroom was laid out.

A glance at his watch told him he was still ahead of schedule, but his cushion had shrunk to several minutes. Inspecting each room was not an option. He was running out of time.

On a hunch, he ignored the next series of unopened doors and instead followed the twisting hallways of the maze all the way to their end. There, past the last flickering candlelight, at the end of a hallway with no other way out, stood the last mahogany door. As with the others, the door showed no sign or number.

When he opened the door to the L-shaped room, his heart skipped a beat. A side view of a throne, similar to the throne from the Midsummer Night's Dream party, greeted him. This throne, however, was an indoor version, upholstered in fabric.

It was the sort of throne the master of the house might use to view his favorite possession. Yet the walls to the side of, and behind, the throne were bare.

This room held only one work of art. And whatever artwork was in the room was on the wall facing the throne, the wall at the end of the L-shape, the wall that was out of Quinn's view.

In three long steps, he stood next to the throne and looked over at the wall.

Found her. His heart pounded.

The painting was lit by an array of soft LED lights recessed into the ceiling above. The rest of the room was dark.

Still ahead of schedule, his watch told him. There was time to take a few seconds to see this babe that men wanted so much. Step closer and check her out.

He drew his breath.

She's a beauty, all right. Someone you really want to know. Whatever the word for "hottie" was that long ago, she's it. Those eyes.

Those eyes.

They look right through you.

An urge to linger crept over him. Why not? He could spare a few more seconds.

Complete the damn mission. He shook his head clear and walked to the corner of the wall displaying the painting.

Flattening himself against the wall, he looked to his side. The motion sensor, a small piece of white plastic perhaps three inches square, was mounted on the top of the wood frame.

The sensor was his first prey. He crept along the wall toward it, his eyes fixed on the tiny lens at the top.

Cybersecurity could do nothing about these independent motion sensors. They were set to go off as soon as the artwork was moved, and they used wireless transmitters that could go anywhere—to the control room or even to someone's cell phone. He would have to disable this sensor himself.

The infrared motion sensor responded to changes in temperature, not movement. It was the abrupt change from the human's body heat the sensor reacted to when the object was moved. If the sensor lens were blocked from changes in temperature, the sensor would not detect any movement.

Clinging to the wall like a spider, he edged toward the

painting. The lens of the sensor glinted in the cool light of an LED spot recessed in the ceiling.

To avoid being set off by innocent passersby, the sensor would have a range extending about a foot out from the painting. Quinn was now approaching that range. He stopped and, from his vest pocket, removed a plastic case containing a small vial. He checked the vial's dual temperature gauges, which showed both the room temperature and the temperature of the vial's contents. The readings were identical.

He unscrewed the top of the vial and brought the vial over above the top of the sensor, out of range of the lens. Holding his breath, he turned the vial on its side and sprayed its aerosolized contents on the top of the sensor.

He watched as the liquid covered all sides of the sensor. The stuff was a moving object but of identical temperature, and would be unnoticed by the sensor. When the liquid solidified, the sensor would no longer detect any temperature change, and would no longer detect movement.

The chemicals needed two minutes to solidify. Still flattened against the wall, he stared at his watch, counting the seconds.

The image of the painting flashed back into his mind. He found himself drawn to it. Had Professor Hale said something about a delayed reaction?

He cleared his mind of the thought and checked the time on his watch. The two minutes were almost up. After allowing an extra thirty seconds of drying time, he looked over at the sensor.

The glue-like mixture had solidified on all sides. Like the prehistoric insect preserved in amber, the motion sensor was now frozen in time and temperature. An earthquake could go undetected by the sensor.

Quinn walked in front of the painting. He laid the quiver on the floor and, from a vest pouch, removed and opened his Leatherman utility knife.

He forced himself to ignore the painting and focus solely on completion of his mission. The steel knife blade glinted in the spotlight as it pierced the upper right corner of the canvas. Quinn sliced down to the bottom of the frame, then over, then up and across, his eyes focused on making clean cuts.

In seconds the painting was out of its frame and lying on the marble floor. He unlocked the quiver's cap and removed several sheets of glassine art paper. Placing the painting between the sheets of art paper, he rolled it up, placed it in the quiver, and locked the cap. He slung the quiver over his shoulder and tightened the strap, then folded the knife and put it back in his vest pouch.

His heart racing, he retraced his steps along the maze of hallways with nameless mahogany doors and flickering candlelight. In moments he was back in the main showroom. He walked across the polished marble floor, ignoring the art treasures hanging all around him.

His rope was still hanging down from the ceiling vent. He glanced at his watch. Still ahead of schedule. The crawl back would go much quicker now that he knew the way.

He tugged hard on the rope. It held firm. He grabbed hold with his other hand and looked up into the waiting attic.

A mocking voice resonated throughout the showroom.

"You're a bit early for your morning appointment, aren't you?"

CHAPTER 30

Newport Shores, California

FLANKED BY TWO GUARDS HOLDING AK-47S, MARCO WALKED from the foyer into the gallery showroom.

His facial expression was cold and composed, the eyes intense with concentration. None of the symptoms of the drug and alcohol intoxication remained. He no longer wore the purple cloak, but he still had on his black shirt and leggings from the party. The sword hung by his side, sheathed in its scabbard.

And his right hand held a 9mm Beretta aimed at Quinn's chest.

The two guards stayed by Marco's side. They stood in a balanced, shooter's stance, feet shoulder-width apart, the twin barrels of the guns pointed at Quinn.

A burst of rapid Italian from Marco echoed in the showroom, and the two guards sprang into action. Quinn raised his arms in the air as one guard removed his gun from its holster and the quiver from his shoulder. The other guard disappeared into the hallway.

The first guard emptied the clip from Quinn's gun and checked for a round in the chamber. The guard handed the clip to Marco and placed Quinn's empty 9mm on the mahogany table in the foyer. After placing the quiver on the floor next to Marco, the guard patted Quinn down, removing the contents from Quinn's vest pouches.

One by one, the incriminating items—the spare clip, the head lamp, the bolt cutters, the knife—were laid in a row on the marble floor. As the first guard was laying out the items, the second guard came jogging back into the showroom. He held the motion sensor that had been on the back of the painting's frame.

"Solo la signorina," said the guard, handing the plastic sensor to his superior.

"Interessante." Marco turned the sensor over in his free hand, examining the clear, solid coating that covered all sides.

"Imaginative." His fingers rubbed the sides. "You are more resourceful than the average thief. But not resourceful enough. There were additional sensors in the frame itself, Mr. Quinn. Tiny little wires, smaller than a hair, set to send an alarm as soon as the canvas was cut from the frame. So, you see, your little plan never had a chance."

Marco handed the plastic sensor back to the guard, who then handed Marco a tablet computer. With his thumb, Marco scrolled through a series of screens showing video surveillance of various areas of the Palazzo. He stopped at one screen.

"A shame, really. Such a shame." He shook his head from side to side as he tilted the tablet to show Quinn the screen. The display showed a real-time picture of Heather, curled up asleep in her bed, her thick braids splayed across her pillow.

"You could have had a wonderful night if you had just stayed with the lovely young lady in her room." Marco looked at the picture. "Such a pretty little *cagna*. You should have availed yourself of the opportunity. You could be making sweet love to her at this moment. Or perhaps be asleep with her in your arms.

"And now, such a mess you are in, eh? You will have, however, a chance at an explanation." The Beretta barrel remained pointed at Quinn's chest. "I am curious as to what you have to say."

Quinn had sketched out a cover story during the crawl through the attic. Its flaws seemed glaring as his words came out.

"One of my clients wanted the painting, a collector for whom money is no object. He offered me so much for the job, I couldn't turn it down."

The corners of Marco's lips turned down in disbelief.

"We can make this go away," Quinn continued. "I'll tell my client I had to abort the mission, that your gallery was too secure. I walk out of here, and in exchange I'll use my connections to obtain for you some of the most valuable artworks in the world, no questions asked. I won't breathe a word of this to anyone."

Marco was silent for a moment, then spoke. "You are correct, Mr. Quinn, that you won't breathe a word of this to anyone. But I'm afraid our business relationship is terminated."

Marco glanced at the tablet computer, scrolling through a series of screens showing the video surveillance of the art gallery. "And I do not believe your story that you were working on behalf of one person, this 'client' art collector of yours. I am not a believer in coincidences to begin with, and let us just say a great deal has happened today. On top of that, no mere collector could have penetrated our security system to such a remarkable extent.

"No, Mr. Quinn. There is much more going on here. You are working for a powerful organization, one with considerable resources. Therefore, the question that is important to me is: Who are *they*?"

Pools of sweat formed under Quinn's arms. He had underestimated Marco.

"You do understand, Mr. Quinn, that tonight you are going to die? That this is the last night of your life? If you cooperate and tell me everything you know about whom you are really working for, then your death will be merciful. You will simply drift into a peaceful sleep. I promise.

"If you do not cooperate, then we will cause you such agony that you will beg on your knees to be allowed to die. I promise that as well. Surely an intelligent man like you can discern the wiser choice, eh?"

Quinn's mouth was dry. He licked his lips and swallowed, his mind searching for a new angle.

"Marco, if I disappear, a lot of people are going to come looking for me."

"Ah, but you shall not disappear, Mr. Quinn." Marco raised his eyebrows and spoke as if he were a professor answering a foolish question from a student.

"Your body will be found tomorrow morning, on the rocks at the bottom of a cliff that overlooks the beautiful Pacific Ocean. You became quite intoxicated at our Midsummer Night's Dream party, you see, and in the middle of the night, you apparently decided to go for a stroll on the grounds. You climbed over the fence bordering the bluff and then fell to your death. The coroner's autopsy will reveal quite a large consumption of alcohol and drugs. An unfortunate and tragic accident to happen to one of our honored guests, but of course we knew nothing."

In his mind's eye, Quinn could see his lifeless body, spread-eagled on the sharp, jagged rocks. The ambulance, the police cars, the jaded detective filling out his report. It would all be quite believable.

Rings of sweat itched at the back of his neck and under his arms. He had one last card to play, and it was a weak one.

"Okay, Marco. Now you leave me no choice. I'm undercover for the feds, in their art crime division. The FBI, Interpol, and DEA all know where I am and have full reports on you. We've been building our case on you for a good while. Not to mention the world of trouble you are in with your superiors at the Societa."

At the last word, Marco's eyes flashed. "I have no superiors *anywhere*, much less with the Societa. I use them for my own ends. Soon enough I will no longer need them at all.

"No one has ever gotten the better of me, Mr. Quinn. Not the Societa lowlifes where I grew up. Not that fanatical Russian; his death brings that rivalry to an end. And certainly not a bumbling American.

"Now you say you are some sort of policeman, eh? My gut tells me you are finally speaking the truth. You have the look and smell of one. What kind—local, national, international—it does not matter. Law enforcement is law enforcement. And you policemen are all the same, with your childish belief that you are fighting for the right against the wrong."

Quinn sensed a chance to buy time by provoking Marco. "We are, Marco. And there's a special section of hell reserved for the thieves of the world. Strip away your Palazzo and your clown clothes and high heels, and that's all you are, you know— a cowardly, naked, little thief."

"*Bastardo!*"

Marco's gun arm lashed out. With a *thwack* the Beretta barrel struck Quinn's jaw.

Bursts of pain exploded like lightning inside Quinn's skull. He staggered sideways. Resisting the urge to fight back, he regained his balance and stood, his head throbbing, his arms still upraised. He licked his lips, tasting the blood trickling down from the corner of his lip.

"Thief, you dare call me?" Marco's voice resonated throughout the room in righteous anger "*I coglioni!* All of history, Mr. Quinn, is the story of the strong taking their rightful spoils from the weak. For centuries, conquering countries have plundered the art of vanquished nations.

"Rome looted Jerusalem. Greece looted Troy. Napoleon looted Egypt. Most of the paintings hanging in your precious museums were stolen from someone! And you have the gall to call *me* a thief!"

Quinn stood still, his eyes flicking between Marco and the guards and the quiver lying on the floor.

"Of all the lies disseminated as opiates to the ignorant masses, Mr. Quinn, surely the most pathetic is that of 'right and wrong.' It is the lie of all lies. And it is used to make cannon fodder out of simple-minded policemen such as you."

With his free hand, Marco made a sweeping gesture toward the showroom. "In this world there *is* no right and wrong. The world just is. And the only way to succeed in this world is to use force. Force to take what you want, whether it is a beautiful woman or a beautiful work of art."

He placed his boot heel on the steel quiver lying on the floor. The Beretta barrel rose again until it was pointing at Quinn's heart.

"Now I have what I have wanted most. And you will go to

your death tonight, Mr. Quinn, knowing that I will have her forever."

Quinn remained motionless, his right wrist turned so that he could keep a steady eye on his watch dial.

The dial flashed once, a soft blue flash, and the entire room was plunged into darkness.

CHAPTER 31

Newport Shores, California

QUINN DOVE BETWEEN MARCO AND THE GUARD STANDING TO Marco's right.

The bright yellow light of muzzle flash flickered above him, and the twin AK-47s blasted the area where he had been standing. Landing on all fours, Quinn reached up with his right hand and grabbed Marco's gun hand at the wrist. At the same time, his left hand reached up and felt for the waist of the guard next to Marco. Quinn's arm snaked around the guard's waist and shoved the guard's belly against the barrel of Marco's gun.

"Drop the gun, Marco!" Quinn pressed the guard's belly harder against Marco's gun barrel.

The gamble worked. Marco fired, pumping three quick bullets into what Marco had believed to be Quinn's stomach, but was the guard's stomach. The wounded guard squealed something in Italian. His AK-47 clattered to the floor.

Still holding on to Marco's wrist, Quinn now twisted it to the side. Marco grunted as his Beretta fell to the tile floor.

Two guns down, one left.

Staccato bursts of gunfire from the remaining AK-47 rang through the air. The other guard, not knowing what else to do, had stepped away and fired at where Quinn had been standing.

Looking down so that the muzzle flashes didn't blind what little night vision he had, Quinn dropped flat to the floor, twisting Marco's wrist farther, pulling Marco off balance and down with him. Marco grunted and fell over sideways, his heavy body landing half on top of Quinn.

With his free arm, Quinn stretched out on the floor under Marco's flailing body and reached around in the darkness for the steel touch of the quiver.

His hand swept back and forth on the tile. There. The quiver had rolled over a few feet from where it had been under Marco's boot. Quinn let go of Marco's wrist and, with both hands, grabbed the quiver and held it against his chest. He rolled over on the hard floor, away from Marco, until he collided with the wall where the entry door was. Scrambling into a crouch, one arm pressing the quiver to his chest, he moved his free hand along the wall, feeling for the cold steel of the door.

AK-47 fire filled the air again, the bullets flying across the room in the general direction of where Quinn had been standing. Marco's voice, somewhere several feet away, shouted in Italian to stop shooting, that they were being tricked into shooting one another.

The bullets fell silent. The only sound in the room was the faint breathing of the wounded guard, who sounded like he was lying on the floor somewhere close by.

Quinn was still crouched, feeling along the wall for the entry door, when something hard hit him across his back with tremendous force, knocking him face down onto the marble floor. His arm wrapped around the quiver braced his fall. As he hit the ground, he twisted his head to the side to see in the darkness.

His free hand landed on something soft, something covered in a warm pool of sticky liquid. It was the stomach of the wounded guard, who was now still, no longer making breathing noises. A few inches away from Quinn's face, a loud clang sounded as whatever had hit Quinn glanced off the floor. From the solid ring of the metal, it had to be Marco's sword.

A boot pressed on his back. The air fluttered with the faint rushing sound of movement. In his mind's eye, Quinn visualized the sword being raised up for a kill stroke. He rolled over on his back and away from Marco's boot. His free hand grabbed hold of the boot and felt up the calf for the leg's position.

The angle of the leg told him that Marco stood with his legs straddled apart, balancing himself for the downward sword-stroke. The split second while Marco paused to figure out Quinn's new location was all the time needed. Quinn grabbed the quiver with both hands and shoved the steel tube straight up between the straddled legs.

There was a *thunk* as the steel cylinder rammed hard into Marco's crotch. A squeal of raw pain cut through the darkness. Loud clangs resonated as the sword fell to the floor.

Cradling the quiver in his arms, Quinn rolled over on the floor until he again hit the wall. He strapped the quiver on his back and with both hands felt along the wall for the steel door. Behind him, Marco groaned and the remaining guard jabbered something in Italian.

Panic rose in his gut as his hands felt along the wall and precious seconds passed. He could try to find the wounded guard's AK-47 and spray the room with gunfire, neutralizing Marco and the guard. Then he would have a weapon to take with him.

But his right hand found the steel door, and then the handle. The door was unlocked. He depressed the thick lever and pulled the heavy door open.

Marco, reacting to the solid metallic sound of the door opening, shouted new instructions to the guard. A hand grabbed at Quinn's neck, missed, and then grabbed at the quiver's strap.

Jerking his body side-to-side, flailing backward with his elbows, Quinn shook off the grasping hand and dove headfirst through the open doorway. He landed hard on the marble floor of the dark hallway. AK-47 fire sprayed from left to right a few feet over his head, thudding into the drywall on the opposite side of the hall.

As he rolled to his right, the bullets ricocheted off the marble floor where he had just landed. He sprang to his feet and zigzagged down the dark hallway at top speed, aiming for the faint outline of the glass window in the hall door, which led to the stairway. Behind him, Marco cursed in Italian and the guard shouted back that he couldn't see.

AK-47 gunfire blasted the marble floor a few yards in back of him, and then hit the wall to his right, much closer.

Then he was through the door and into the stairway at the end of the hall. He had taken a step and jumped down to the first landing when the glass window in the stairway door shattered into pieces and bullets clanged into the metal body of the door.

His heart hammering his chest, Quinn half ran, half jumped down the darkened stairway, putting his hands out in front of him and bouncing his body off the walls at each landing. Above him the stairway echoed with shouts and bursts of gunfire. Then he was through the last stairway door and into the quiet of the parking garage.

In the windowless garage, his eyes found the red-and-white

exit sign, the sign he had noted during his Palazzo tour with Sienna. The simple, glow-in-the-dark sign hung over the exit door as a backup in case of a power failure. He sprinted across the white-tiled floor, bounded up the steps, flung open the door, and ran outside into the night.

CHAPTER 32

Newport Shores, California

WITHOUT PAUSING, QUINN SET OUT AT A FULL SPRINT ACROSS the damp lawn, making a straight line for the side gate.

Though the power was still out throughout the grounds of the Palazzo, and clouds still blanketed the sky, his eyes adjusted to the ambient light from the moon and stars. To his right he could make out the black shape of the two-story maintenance building, and in front of him the outline of the Italian cypresses and the black fence with the side gate.

The intermittent rain had stopped again. The only sounds were the rasping rhythm of his breath and the rapid thump of his footsteps on the lawn.

How many seconds did he have until he was a well-lit target? Cybersecurity had succeeded in shutting off all electrical power going into the Palazzo, and had done what they could to jam the software that activated the backup generators. But they could do nothing to stop the backup generators themselves, which were self-contained. He had been told to expect a few minutes at most, until someone manually turned on the backup generators that, whether they were battery- or gas-powered, were sure to be state-of-the-art.

With the original plan, a few minutes would have been plenty of time. He would have hidden in the garage until the power outage, then sprinted across the lawn to the gate.

Now he was running for his life. To his right noises came from the maintenance building. Flashlight beams moved in the dark second-story windows. Behind him shouts rang out from the Palazzo, followed by doors slamming and the pounding of feet on the stairs.

The side gate was coming up fast. The steel coils of razor wire, protruding from the end of the row of Italian cypresses where the fence met the gate, glinted in the moonlight.

He had selected his escape route during Sienna's tour of the Palazzo grounds. Between the fence and the side gate, he had noticed a gap between their two coils of razor wire. The gap wasn't more than a foot wide, but was helped by the fact that the gate was shorter than the fence, making the gap of uneven height. It would be a tight fit, but it would have to do.

As he drew closer, he focused on the narrow slice of space. His only way out.

He was about a dozen steps away from the gate when the power from the backup generators came on.

The entire grounds of the Palazzo were lit with thousands of watts of floodlights. In the harsh light Quinn now saw himself, his forearms pumping furiously back and forth, his feet a blur beneath him. The floodlights turned him into an open invitation to any gunman within range.

Ahead of him, the coach light atop the end of the stone wall flared on, the silvery barbs of the razor wire glittering in the incandescence. Behind him garage doors rattled open and automobile engines revved. A burst of automatic weapons fire hit somewhere to his left, then again, closer.

Four steps, three steps, two.

In a running jump, he braced both feet against the gate, one hand grabbing the top of the gatepost, the other hand wrapped around the last finial of the fence, less than an inch from the coil of razor wire. With a grunt, he swung his legs in an arc up and over the gate, watching the coils of razor wire loom up at him as his body just cleared the long shiny barbs.

For a split second, he braced his feet on the other side of the gate, half expecting to be struck by a fusillade from a dozen rifles. Then he let go and sprang backward, lifting his arms high to clear the coils of wire. He hit the ground on his side, rolled once, then sprang into a runner's crouch, the steel quiver banging against his back.

Above him, multiple rounds of gunfire sprayed the area where he had jumped. He had been a precious freaking second ahead of the hunt. Bullets pinged off the gate and fence, sending tiny fragments of metal over his head. With a loud *pop*, the coach light burst into a thousand shards of glass.

Quinn sprinted across the driveway, vaulted over the six-foot stone wall on the other side, and landed in the relative safety of the grounds of the vacant mansion adjacent to the Palazzo.

During the long hours of surveillance he had spent on the mansion's rooftop, he had committed to memory practically every tree, bush, and blade of grass along what was to be his escape route. That effort paid off as he sprinted along the dark grounds of the estate, past the empty pool, past the gardener's shed. He ran toward a copse of overgrown trees near the mansion's entrance to the private road.

Behind him the shooting had stopped, replaced by a babble of voices shouting in Italian and the rumble of automobile engines. Though his lungs felt like they were bursting, he kept running at full speed until he reached the cover of the trees.

The innocent-looking branches were still in their pile atop the wet canvas cover. Underneath the canvas cover, his BMW motorcycle waited for him. He swung his leg over the seat and felt for the starter button. Then he forced himself to pause.

The rumble of the SUVs sounded close by, on the other side of the stone wall. Quick mental math told him he would never make it out alive.

The original plan had called for him to roll his bike from its hiding place on the grounds of the vacant mansion and out onto the private road. When he was far enough away, he would start the engine and motor away down Coral Cove Lane. Now, with the guards alerted at the main gate and a convoy of SUVs after him, he would be a sitting duck the moment he emerged onto the road.

He dismounted and reached into the bike's saddlebag. He removed the spare 9mm and tucked it into his holster, then removed hand grenades and smoke grenades, inserting them into separate vest pouches.

Staying low to the ground, he scrambled along the wall until he was opposite the Palazzo's main gate. The rumble of the SUVs was louder. The voices of men shouting in Italian rose above the engine noise. Holding his breath, he risked a quick glimpse over the wall.

The Palazzo's main gate was fully lit. A guard stood outside the guardhouse, brandishing an assault rifle. The guard was talking to two men in the front seats of an SUV idling at the entrance. Each man in the front seat held a rifle with the barrel sticking out of the open car window. Behind the front vehicle were two more SUVs.

Quinn crouched against the wall, his mind racing. The private road was still the only way out.

The SUVs were the ones from the convoy that had survived Orlov's attack. He remembered how they had been reinforced against bullets. A strike would have to aim at their undercarriage. He pulled the two smoke grenades out of his pocket.

Pulling the igniter rings, he lobbed them over the wall, one on the far side of the gate and one on the near side.

Two seconds later consecutive bangs echoed in the night. Clouds of thick, black smoke arose on the other side of the wall. Panicked shouts came from the guards, followed by the sounds of car doors slamming and footsteps. The men were abandoning their vehicles.

He already had the first hand grenade out. Gripping the safety lever in place with his throwing hand, he grabbed the pull-ring with his index finger, twisted it, and pulled it out. With a measured side throw, he lobbed the grenade over the wall so that it would roll underneath the first SUV. Without waiting he scrambled farther back along the wall, stopping twice to toss the other two grenades under the other two SUVs.

Keeping his head down, he sprinted back to his waiting BMW. Just he swung his leg over the seat, three consecutive bangs came from the other side of the wall, followed by a deeper boom—probably one of the gas tanks.

The bike fired up as soon as he pressed the starter button and growled in first gear as he maneuvered through the trees. He pulled onto the asphalt of the private road, then noticed a bright reflection in his side mirrors.

The entrance gate to the Palazzo was one massive conflagration. All three SUVs were on fire, and chunks of burning wreckage were scattered across the driveway. Bright yellow and orange flames lapped up the spilled fuel oozing down the driveway, sending up clouds of thick, oily smoke to mix with the smoke still spewing from the smoke grenades.

As the BMW rocketed down the road, behind him came the boom of another explosion, and in the vibrating mirrors, balls of yellow-black fire arose from the hindmost SUV.

The stately homes of Coral Cove Lane were a blur as the bike raced along quiet residential streets. The BMW turned a corner, and Quinn noticed the quiver banging against the side of his bike. The strap was coming loose.

He pulled over under a streetlight. He had traveled at least six or seven blocks from the private road, and even if other SUVs came after him, nothing was making it through the burning conflagration that blocked the Palazzo driveway.

His bike purred in neutral as he tightened the strap so that the quiver was secured against his back. Couldn't risk losing his precious cargo. A glance in his mirrors revealed nothing but a quiet street of elegant homes.

Drops of water splashed on his mirrors, misting over the images of the homes. The rain was falling again. Quinn put his hands on the handlebars and his foot on the gearshift lever.

A loud whine punctured the solitude. He jerked his head up. The reflection of a headlight appeared in his left mirror, and there was a sharp crack from the white mailbox of the house nearest him. Small pieces of its white-painted metal flew into the air like shrapnel.

He yanked the bike to the middle of the road, and his hand twisted the throttle. As the BMW accelerated down the street, the yellow headlight in his mirror grew larger.

In the warm glow of the streetlights, he saw the color of the bike behind the oncoming headlight. There was no mistaking the bright red Ducati from the Palazzo garage.

Marco was coming up fast.

CHAPTER 33

Newport Shores, California

THE BMW ROARED THROUGH THE REMAINING TURNS OF Newport Shores, and suddenly Quinn found himself speeding up to the red-light intersection with Pacific Coast Highway.

He had gained a few yards on Marco, but in his side mirror was the Ducati headlight coming around the corner.

The highway before him was deserted. Quinn twisted the throttle, and the BMW shot into the intersection and turned left. His best chance to lose Marco would be in the hills of Laguna Beach, in the crazy quilt of winding, narrow streets.

On the open highway, a heavy downpour pelted his face and soaked his hair. Strong winds blowing in from the sea buffeted the BMW as it sped down the desolate stretch of road bracketed by wilderness on one side and ocean on the other.

The bike rounded a bend, and the lights of Laguna loomed ahead, blurring through the veil of rain. Running through the empty, red-light intersection at Broadway, Quinn turned left, roared past the darkened shops and restaurants of downtown, and zigzagged his way up into the hills.

Right, left, right, left—a maze of streets with exotic names like Mystic Way and Driftwood Bay. Quinn took the turns as sharply as he dared, his knee almost scraping the street as he rounded the corners. The headlight from the Ducati stayed constant in his side mirror, disappearing after each turn and then reappearing.

The driving rain formed puddles in the narrow streets, puddles that could cause skidding and could hide dangerous potholes. At the next corner, the sloping streets were joined by a pool of rainwater that stretched across the entire width of the road. It was impossible to tell how deep it was or what it hid. Quinn was forced to slow down for the turn. As his BMW splashed through the water, a gunshot sounded above the storm noise, and the side mirror of the parked car to his right exploded in pieces.

Marco hadn't missed by much. Quinn thought of the framed motorcycle-racing photographs in the Palazzo garage. His pursuer was an expert rider, skilled in dealing with high speeds and adverse conditions.

Quinn took the next few turns in rapid succession, but after each turn the yellow Ducati headlight reappeared in his side mirror. He hadn't lost any ground to Marco, but he hadn't gained any either. To have a chance of getting away, he somehow needed to put the Ducati at least two streets back.

As the BMW accelerated past a turn, Quinn noticed on his left a flight of concrete stairs bordered by metal handrails. At the top of the stairs, pouring rain bounced off what looked like a flat concrete pad. Guessing that the steps led to another side street and desperate for something that would give him an edge, Quinn veered to his left and aimed the bike up the stairs.

Lifting his seat up, he balanced his body forward, as if he

were riding a bucking bronco. Then he twisted the throttle and tore up the stairs. He had to climb fast enough that Marco wouldn't have time to stop at the base of the stairs and take a shot. The engine howled, and the bike's body shuddered in protest, but the BMW charged up the concrete steps as if it had been launched. The quiver banged all over his back, and his bones jolted as if they might separate, but he held steady.

The top of the stairs was coming up fast. He strained to see what was ahead, but all he saw was the flat concrete pad at the top. His headlight shone on the pouring rain, the raindrops bouncing off the concrete, and nothing but darkness beyond. Holding his breath, half expecting a bullet to slam into his back, he shot over the top and onto the concrete pad.

The bike bounced once, then held, and shot forward on the slick concrete. Quinn looked ahead, then left and right, expecting the lampposts of a street with cars and houses. Ahead lay only darkness, darkness in front and to the sides, darkness with rain pouring down but not bouncing off a street, not bouncing off anything. Then the concrete pad disappeared beneath him, and darkness was everywhere.

He was airborne.

CHAPTER 34

Laguna Beach, California

AS THE BIKE FLEW FORWARD INTO THE DARKNESS, QUINN FELT AS
if he were floating in some sort of invisible sea. With blackness
on all sides, vertigo set in, removing his perception of space and
position.

Then the bike descended, and the wind roared in his ears.
His spatial orientation returned. He gripped the handlebars as
he squinted down through the rain.

He was falling toward smooth black asphalt. A street? No,
the asphalt bore the straight white lines of a parking lot. Behind
him he glimpsed the bottom of a flight of stairs going up the
side of the concrete pad. The concrete pad had nothing but
steep flights of stairs on both sides. The pad itself was part of a
long, elevated sidewalk leading to something, probably some
sort of scenic viewpoint for tourists.

He shut out all thoughts except for landing. If he skidded
and fell, it would be over. He would be an easy target for a kill
shot from Marco. Holding his breath, he lifted his body up off

the bike to absorb the shock of landing and concentrated on bringing up the front of the bike so that he landed on his rear tire.

With an impact that jarred every bone in his body, the bike's rear tire hit the slick asphalt and shot forward. The bike wobbled, skidding forward on one tire while the handlebars jerked back and forth in his hands. He leaned forward and down until, with another jolt, he brought the front tire to the asphalt.

Now the rear of the bike shimmied from side to side as if it were about to fishtail. Quinn shifted his weight again, kept his seat off the saddle, and focused on getting the bike balanced. The bike stabilized, and he headed across the asphalt and toward the parking lot exit.

In his side-view mirror, the Ducati headlight appeared behind him. Marco was at the top of the stairs, either preparing to ride down or preparing to shoot. Quinn jerked his BMW back and forth on the blacktop, through the parking-lot exit, and onto the street.

It was a wide residential street, sloping downhill. Despite the rain, Quinn opened up the throttle and barreled straight toward the corner. This was the chance he had been waiting for. Marco pausing at the top of the stairs gave him an extra few seconds for a getaway, a chance to put enough twists and turns behind him to lose the Ducati.

As he turned the corner, Quinn decided to head back toward the highway, where he could open the throttle up and lose his pursuer in a burst of sheer speed. Right, left, right, left. He cut through the narrow streets until he reached Laguna Canyon, where he turned west and headed toward the coast and the open highway.

The rain was now a full-fledged storm. Without the protection of buildings, the gusts of wind blowing in from the sea were like invisible punches, pushing him back and to the sides, forcing him to go slower. Rainwater from overflowing gutters streamed down both sides of Laguna Canyon. Puddles and pools were everywhere, their oil-slick surfaces shining fluorescent in the blurry glow of the streetlights.

He glanced at his side mirrors. No sign of the Ducati.

To the sides, the darkened shops and restaurants of downtown Laguna passed by in slow motion. An Italian restaurant, an upscale sushi bar, a downscale Irish pub. On the right were the empty grounds of the Festival of Arts, with a colorful sign advertising the Pageant of the Masters. Through the gray curtain of rain, a red light shone up ahead. It was the intersection with the highway.

Adrenaline surging through his veins, Quinn maneuvered around a curb-high semicircle of rippling water covering a flooded gutter, and turned the corner onto the highway.

With the heavy storm and the late hour, Pacific Coast Highway was as deserted as before. The motels and apartment buildings on the beach side of the road provided some protection from the wind. He leaned forward, trying to meld his body into one with the machine, and twisted the throttle.

In a few blocks, he was past the city limits and lights of civilization. Now the buildings on the sides were gone, and he was exposed to the full force of the storm. The wind pummeled his bike with the force of a hurricane, and the raindrops stung his face like hail. The wind-driven cold soaked his clothing, and his hands shook as he gripped the handlebars.

Coming up around the next bend was a two-lane road that branched off from the highway and into the wilderness preserve. He remembered that the road curved up and over the highway, with the steep, mountain-like slopes of the wilderness preserve on the right and a sheer drop to the ocean on the left. The road was seldom used, as it was designed only for recreational visitors to the preserve. Even if Marco knew about this road, the odds were he would shoot right past it, thinking Quinn had kept to the highway.

It was his best chance to get away. He flicked the bike over, slowed down to twenty miles per hour, and rode onto the two-lane road.

The gray, chained, steel gate of the closed entrance loomed ahead of him. When he reached the gate, he brought the bike to a stop.

Standing with his feet on the ground, he inched the bike around the gatepost next to the steep dirt slope. Ahead of him, the bike's headlight shone on muddy water pouring down the narrow road. The asphalt was potholed and cracked, and with the pounding from the fierce storm, dirt and rocks were trickling down from the slope. He would have to take it slow.

Past the gate, he brought the bike's speed back up to twenty. Staying in the center of the road, he kept an eye out for rocks and debris. To his right was the almost total blackness of the slope's steep earthen face. To his left the sky was a mass of gray-black clouds. Just over the guardrail, he caught glimpses of the storm-tossed sea. This road, he remembered, made a long loop through the preserve and exited out back at the highway.

One bend, two bends. His pace was slow, but if Marco had missed the turnoff, it didn't matter. Shivering, he concentrated on keeping the bike in the center of the road. All he had to do was keep going.

With each bend in the road his confidence grew. He must have eluded Marco back in Laguna Beach. When this road let him back out onto the highway, he would be well past Newport Shores, and on his way home. He brought the bike's speed up to forty.

A roaring noise behind him drowned out the storm. The back of his BMW lifted up in the air, and a series of hard thumps slammed into his back. He ducked, trying to protect his head and neck, thinking of the bulletproof layering in his vest.

The back of his BMW came back down hard, and the bike wobbled, the rear tire in shreds. Quinn braked and twisted the throttle back, trying to regain control of the machine. Then the remaining pieces of tire flew off, and his back wheel was on its rim, the metal shrieking and sparking against the asphalt.

The bike leaned hard to the right, too far to pull back up. The only option was to lay it down and try to ride it out as the bike slowed. Holding on to the handlebars, Quinn scrambled to position himself on top as the bike slid forward on the road.

More hard thumps hit him in the back. Bullets clanged into the body of the bike, and his left leg stung in several places. The bike was out of control and sliding toward the hillside. He jumped off the BMW and tucked into a body roll, protecting his head with his arms.

His body hit the asphalt with a force that knocked the wind out of him and flayed chunks of fabric off his vest and slices of skin off his back. He bounced once, then hit the ground hard and rolled over and over until he slammed into the guardrail.

CHAPTER 35

Newport Shores, California

HE COUGHED UP MUDDY WATER AND OPENED HIS EYES.

Cold water flowed over his head and shoulders, little waves splashing onto his face. He was lying on his back next to the guardrail in a stream of water running down the road.

He turned to his side and out of the stream, coughing up more water. As he moved, darts of pain stung every nerve in his body. Realizing he must have slipped out of consciousness, he looked around to identify his surroundings and orient himself.

The storm was still raging. Rain pelted the ground, and the wind blew it in wild gusts against the earthen slope on the far side of the road.

Several yards up the road, the wreck of his BMW lay close to the mountain side of the road, the mangled bare rim of the rear wheel sticking up. The bike had slid to a stop, facing backward, its still-working headlight illuminating the road. Wisps of steam rose from the warm engine as the raindrops bounced off the steel cover.

He hadn't been unconscious for long. Perhaps only seconds.

His head throbbed, his ears were ringing, and his body hurt in countless places. The lacerations on his back where the clothing had been flayed off stung as if the skin had been stabbed with needles. His left leg felt like it was on fire. With his hand, he reached down and felt the sticky blood that oozed from the bullet wounds in his thigh.

He reached in his holster for his 9mm. Gone, either lying somewhere on the rain-swept road or at the bottom of the ocean on the other side of the guardrail. The quiver strap was no longer across his chest. Ignoring the shooting pains in his shoulder, he reached in back for the steel tube. Gone as well.

There, at the edge of the BMW headlight beam. The black steel tube was on the other side of the road, intact and lying in mud against the steep earthen slope. It must have come off when he jumped and rolled. Raindrops bounced off the metal.

A new sound penetrated through the storm. Unknown, yet vaguely familiar.

He closed his eyes and focused on separating the various sounds around him. The wind from the storm was a loud rushing sound, rising and falling in pitch with the speed of the gusts. The pouring rain was a drumbeat on the asphalt, changing its sound only when a gust of wind blew it sideways. The muddy stream next to him was a steady gurgle.

The other sound drew closer. It was more of a whirring noise. Rhythmic. It was north of him, and to the west.

Chrr-chrr-chrr.

With a jolt of recognition, Quinn lifted up his head and looked over the guardrail and out to sea.

The lone helicopter circled over the ocean, heading toward the road. There were no markings on the chopper, civilian or military, and it was black, as if designed for night maneuvers. He didn't recognize the type. It was about the size of a Little

Bird, or maybe a commercial helo that had been modified. Through the rain Quinn could make out the twin 7.65mm machine guns mounted on the sides.

The guns that minutes earlier had blasted away at him, knocking him off his bike.

Whoever was in the chopper thought they had killed him. They might be circling back to make sure. He needed to play dead. Laying his head back down, he angled his body so that he could see the helo if it came near the road. Shivering in the cold and rain, he lay in place and waited.

The *chrr-chrr-chrr* became louder, and the helo moved into his field of vision. It hovered over the road a few yards ahead of his wrecked BMW.

A floodlight on the bottom of the helicopter flicked on, shining a bright beam of light on a circle of the road north of the BMW. The passenger door opened, and Quinn made out the silhouettes of two figures inside, the pilot and a passenger. A steel cable ladder dropped down from the door and hung in the beam of the floodlight, the end dangling just above the road.

The pilot was performing a difficult maneuver, trying to keep the helicopter stationary over the narrow road while it was being buffeted by the driving winds and rain, and at the same time keeping the rotor blades a safe distance from the earthen slope. The road didn't have enough room to land. Past the guardrail, it was a sheer hundred-yard drop down a cliff face to the stormy sea below.

The passenger leaned out of the helicopter, turned around, and began to climb down the ladder. Through the driving rain, only the silhouette of the man was visible.

The helicopter swayed in the storm, and this in turn made the ladder swing back and forth. About a third of the way down, the man stopped his descent, shouting and motioning at the pilot, who gestured in response.

The pilot was having difficulty keeping the helo in place. He had to position the chopper to hover diagonally over the two-lane road, as the aircraft was longer than the road was wide, and the width of the rotor blades was as wide as the road itself. The position of the ladder had an even smaller margin of error. If the chopper moved several feet to the left, the ladder would be hanging over the ocean. If it moved a few feet to the right, the rotor blades would be slicing into the steep hillside on the other side of the road.

The man resumed climbing down the ladder, taking one rung at a time. He wore black boots and goggles and a black coat. When he reached the bottom of the ladder, the man hung for a moment with his feet in the air and his back to Quinn. Then he dropped to the ground and turned to face the hillside.

In the intense clarity of the halogen floodlight, the wind-reddened, scowling profile was unmistakable.

Marco.

He had doubled back to the Palazzo and returned with his big guns. With his helicopter, he could follow Quinn anywhere.

Marco ducked down and jogged out of the turbulence kicked up by the rotor wash. At the edge of the floodlight, he stood with his hands clasped behind him. He glanced at Quinn, then at the wrecked BMW, as if admiring his work.

Bareheaded, oblivious to the storm, Marco walked over to the quiver. He bent over and picked up the steel tube.

Lifting his goggles, he examined the tube carefully. He ran his hand along the strap, then swung the quiver over his back. With one hand on the strap, he moved his goggles back into position and walked back toward the waiting ladder.

Quinn lay still, frustrated at his helplessness. Marco hadn't even bothered to carry a weapon. The twin machine guns on the helicopter stood ready to blast away if he so much as moved. He would be riddled with bullets before he could take two steps.

Just outside the circle of rotor wash, Marco stopped. He shouted at the pilot and pointed at the hillside. The pilot nodded his head and reached for the control panel. Marco walked around the rotor wash, past the ladder, and over to the guardrail at the edge of the road.

The helicopter moved away from the road until it was well over the sea. It was maneuvering in preparation for something. But what?

Two bright flashes of yellow fire from the sides of the helicopter streaked through the night and, with a boom, exploded into the dirt hillside.

Standing at the edge of the road, Marco pointed farther down the hillside. The helicopter turned and fired again. Two more bright yellow streaks blazed through the darkness. Another boom, and the missiles crashed into the hillside several yards down from where the first two had hit.

Chunks of mud and rock rained down from the slope, thudding into the asphalt. From somewhere higher up the hill, a ten-foot-wide hunk of dirt crashed on top of the BMW, the momentum moving the combined dirt-and-bike mass several feet down the slick asphalt. Rocks and dirt at the bottom of the slope broke loose and slid out into the road.

Quinn looked over at the disintegrating hillside. The logic of the move was brutally efficient. Firing the air-to-ground missiles into the rain-soaked slope was an effective way to eliminate an entire crime scene. Why leave behind a complicated mess with a body, a wrecked vehicle, and hundreds of rounds of ammunition that could be investigated and traced? Why indeed, when you can cause a powerful landslide, exacerbated by a driving storm, which sweeps everything into the raging sea, to be discovered years later, if ever?

A rumbling noise came from across the road. Large cracks had formed in the hillside, sending more chunks of earth down onto the road.

The rotor noise came closer. The helicopter maneuvered back into position over the road. Marco grabbed the hanging steel ladder and placed one foot on the bottom rung.

CHAPTER 36

Newport Shores, California

As carefully as he had descended the ladder, Marco began his ascent.

He placed one foot at a time on a rung, and waited until both feet were stable before taking the next step. Both hands gripped the steel cables as the ladder twisted in the driving storm.

In the glare of the floodlight, the raindrops splattered and bounced off the slippery steel bars. Marco removed a foot from the second rung and placed it on the third rung.

A blast of wind knocked the helicopter closer to the hillside. Marco paused, bracing his hands and feet as the ladder swung back and forth. The helicopter rocked side to side, the storm fighting the pilot's maneuvers.

Quinn's mind raced. The quiver dangled by its strap, banging into Marco's back. "Fail-secure" was the euphemistic jargon used to sum up the security measures built into the steel tube. At the time, they had all seemed like an afterthought. Now the fail-secure options would be his only chance.

The GPS would track the unit. The secure cap would buy additional time.

But those were all after the fact. He needed to stop Marco now.

Deep cracking sounds came from his right. More fissures had opened up in the rain-soaked hillside. At the base of the hill, a three-foot wall of mud had formed and was spreading across the road.

Fail-secure. A term no doubt dreamed up by a bureaucrat in a cubicle, designed to sound reassuring even if it lent a false sense of safety.

The fail-secure features coalesced into an idea.

To Quinn's knowledge, it had never been tested in the field. It was a long shot at best. But it was the only option. He would have an interesting final report to file. If there was one.

Marco had resumed his climb. Rain pelted him from all sides, and the steel ladder rocked in the wind. Quinn watched as Marco placed a foot on a rung, tugged at the strap to make sure the quiver was still there, then brought up the other foot.

A series of thuds came from the right. Rocks and dirt chunks were falling onto the road. The wall of mud, now larger, was moving slowly across the road toward him.

Marco reached for the fourth rung. Halfway up. The quiver hanging on his back tossed and turned in the winds.

It was time.

Quinn dragged himself sideways to the middle of the road, then crouched on one knee in a spot where he had an uninterrupted line of sight with the helicopter. He hoped Marco and the pilot were far too preoccupied to notice his movement. Open gusts of wind-driven rain slammed into his face, and muddy water splashed onto his chest.

He brought his right wrist up to his face. With his left finger, he rubbed the raindrops off the watch face and felt the buttons around the bezel. Tensing his body in preparation, he glanced at the quiver dangling behind the climbing man.

One freaking chance, and it would have to be done right.

Marco brought his left foot up from the fifth rung to the sixth rung, then moved his left hand up the ladder. With his right hand, he reached up and grabbed the steel handle of the passenger door. Struggling against the buffeting winds, he pulled open the door, preparing to vault himself past the remaining rungs and into the cockpit. As he opened the door, he leaned forward, and the quiver bounced against his back. With his left hand he reached back and grabbed the quiver.

Now.

Quinn staggered to his feet, bracing himself against the storm. He felt for the third button over from the top of the watch bezel. He pressed that button down with his index finger, then with his thumb pressed the bright-red button on the opposite size of the bezel, the button that was labeled GPS but was a transmitter.

The black steel tube sparked with what looked like lightning. The bright, yellow-gold streaks arced between the bottom and top of the tube, then spread up Marco's left arm. The lightning traveled across his body and up his right arm to the steel door handle, and from there onto the metal body of the helicopter and inside to the cockpit.

The circuit was complete. The anti-theft electroshock system in the quiver, a surge of high-voltage electricity, had combined with the rain and steel to turn the tube into an ultra-powerful stun gun.

The force of the electric shock threw Marco's hands and feet off the handle and ladder. He dropped down, but managed to hook his right arm around a middle rung, stopping his fall.

From there he dangled, his legs kicking as the ladder twisted in the wind.

The helicopter tilted to one side and shuddered, then swung across the road. The tips of the rotor blades sliced into the hillside, spinning off chunks of dirt. The bird backed away from the slope, hovering unsteadily. The pilot was trying to stay over the asphalt. Through the open passenger door, the caution lights flashed red and white on the instrument panel. The high voltage had damaged the aircraft's electrical system.

The quiver dangled in the air below Marco. Lightning no longer arced over the ladder and helicopter. Only the black steel tube itself still sparked with electricity.

The electric shock had stopped as soon as the quiver was no longer making contact with Marco's body. The brevity of the massive shock was probably why Marco was still alive.

Unable to stay over the road, the helicopter drifted away from the hillside and over the cliff. Marco clung to the ladder, his arm around the middle rung, the sparking quiver dangling by its strap.

Out over the open sea, the helicopter was hit from all sides by the full force of the storm. Torrents of wind-driven rain pounded the helo to one side, then the other. The aircraft shuddered and jerked upward.

The quiver strap slid off Marco's left shoulder and down his arm. The strap dangled from his wrist, then slid past his grasping fingers and into the air.

Marco reached out with his left hand, managing to grab hold of the tube by one end.

The electric shock from the tube jolted his body for a second time. Bright yellow-gold sparks traveled along his body and up the steel ladder. His arm jerked up, letting go of the quiver.

For a moment, the sparking steel tube seemed to hang in the air. Then it fell toward the sea.

Marco let go of the ladder, kicked off the bottom rung, and dove head first for the quiver. His desperate two-handed grab caught only air. The quiver was already several feet below him as it dropped toward the sea.

The steel tube and the struggling figure fell past the cliff edge and Quinn's line of sight.

How freaking insane. Marco had known that the quiver was still electrified. Even if he had somehow caught the tube, he would have fallen to his death. Yet he had dived for it as if nothing else mattered.

Movement out over the sea caught Quinn's eye. The helicopter, now out of control, circled into a tailspin. The front tilted down, the tail lifted up, and the entire aircraft tilted over almost on its side. The chopper spun around, then dropped straight down toward the sea.

A rumbling noise jerked Quinn's attention back to his right and to the landslide moving across the road. The wall of mud and rocks and debris was now several feet tall and stretched up and down the road as far as he could see. It was moving toward him, and would be on him in seconds. He couldn't even walk, let alone outrun it. His only option was to ride it out.

He staggered over to the guardrail. Its footings might hold up against the landslide. He lay down on the road and wrapped his arms and legs around the guardrail's steel posts.

Metal scraping noises cut through the roar of the mudslide. Several yards up the road, the wall of mud had scooped up the wrecked BMW and turned the motorcycle over as if it was a toy. Then the motorcycle was no more, swallowed up by the moving mass.

Now the roar of the landslide was much louder. The wall of mud was only a few yards away and as tall as a damn house. He tightened his grip on the steel posts. The mud was so close, he could see the individual chunks of rock and wood churning and then disappearing, as if the approaching mass were the jaws of some monstrous creature that devoured everything in its path.

A rumble shook the ground beneath him. Quinn took a deep breath, tucked his head into his chest, and braced himself. Then the mountain of mud and rock hit him with terrific force, and everything went dark.

CHAPTER 37

Laguna Beach, California

HE WAS AGAIN ALONE IN THE ENDLESS BLACK SEA, THE SEA HE HAD last visited during a drunken nightmare in Rome. The darkness was total, but the water was calm and temperate, as if he had found some Caribbean cove located on a distant planet.

Without stars or moon, the night sky above him was as dark as the ocean. He swam a slow freestyle. The only sound was the soft splashing of his legs flutter kicking. On and on, he swam.

Was this the afterlife? If so, he should have done some things differently during his brief mortal life. Yet this place indicated no pain, no misery. Just darkness.

When he turned his head to breathe and opened his eyes, it seemed that the color of the ocean was lightening with each turn. After several strokes the sea had become a battleship gray.

He flipped over on his back and was surprised that the sky had changed color along with the sea. Everything around him was now gray. Curious, he began doing the backstroke, to better see his changing surroundings.

With each stroke, the color of sea and sky continued to lighten. Right stroke, left stroke, and the gray sea and sky lightened to a kind of silver. The silver became a cream, then a milky-white. His arms dipped into a milky-white sea, and he gazed up at a milky-white sky.

Currents of consciousness flowed together, and Quinn opened his eyes, blinked, and then opened them again. The sky became the white hospital ceiling and wall, and the sea became the white hospital sheets that had fallen off his shoulders.

Will stood next to his bed, a smile not quite masking the worried look on his face. Someday, the man's often-wrinkled forehead would become corrugated.

"Finally." The concern in Will's voice showed through the sarcasm.

Quinn tried to speak, but his voice came out as a croak. He licked his lips, swallowed, and tried again.

"How bad?" he rasped.

"Bad enough," replied Will. "You took three rounds in the leg. Parts of your back look like a butcher was interrupted while he was skinning you. The worst, though, was the exposure. According to the doctors, with the trauma and exposure combined, there were times when you probably came close to checking out."

Quinn tried to move the wounded leg under the sheet. Needles of pain shot up his thigh.

"You owe your life to the rain," Will continued. "It poured throughout the night and eventually that ton of mud washed off of you, off the road, and over the cliff. A group of cyclists found you on their Sunday-morning ride into the wilderness preserve. You were wrapped around the guardrail and stone cold. At first they thought you were dead.

"Then they found a pulse and called 911. The paramedics

said prying your fingers off the guardrail footings felt like you had rigor mortis."

"Feels a bit like it now," Quinn rasped, licking his lips.

"Here." Will handed him a chilled bottle of water.

The cold water on his parched throat breathed life into him. In a few gulps, Quinn finished half the bottle. He sighed and leaned his head back on the pillow.

"Bottom line?"

"Bottom line," Will sighed, "no permanent damage that we can see. The bruises and wounds are seriously nasty. But they will heal."

"And the cover story?"

"You will be reported to the media, under a different name, of course, as a hiker who stayed after park closing, lost his way, and luckily survived the storm."

"Good." Quinn thought for a moment. "And cleanup?"

"You've been here a few days, Michael. Cleanup is well under way. Our recovery divers have already turned over Mr. Leone's body to the Laguna authorities. It will be reported that the late Mr. Leone died in an unfortunate helicopter crash. A consequence of unwisely taking his helo for a ride during a fierce storm, late at night, too close to dangerous cliffs. The Laguna police are happy to cooperate. They've had enough excitement for ten summers and would very much like to see this whole matter go away quietly during the height of tourist season.

"As for the rest, the divers from our recovery team retrieved your BMW, so that is off the radar. The helicopter is somewhere at the bottom of the sea, and will stay there."

"Did they find the girl?"

"What girl?"

"That painting of the girl. It was in the quiver. What

happened to her?" Quinn surprised himself that he was even asking this question.

Will looked as if he was now re-appraising Quinn's return to health. He hesitated, then spoke. "Oh, that painting. Right. No longer part of your mission, of course. Well, the quiver itself is missing, and the GPS is inactive. With the storm and the landslide, we had presumed the quiver and its contents were lost at sea. Your story confirms it.

"It's regrettable, naturally, as is any kind of collateral damage. Bad luck for a museum someplace. But I'm sure this painting will turn up some day. If not, well, someone can always paint another one. Right?"

Quinn looked at his friend. "Of course."

"Now, regarding your mission," Will emphasized the last word. "The Director asked me to extend to you his congratulations. Mission accomplished. Mr. Leone's burgeoning heroin empire is out of business as permanently as is the late Mr. Leone. The Societa here in the States seems to have closed up shop and vanished, virtually overnight.

"As a bonus, Interpol and the FBI, called in by the local police after the accident, are reporting that the Palazzo is yielding the greatest recovery of stolen art in modern history. I don't follow that stuff and don't know the details, but apparently they have retrieved something like the top fifty most-wanted stolen artworks in the world. The Director asked me to relay to you Professor Hale's deepest gratitude in that regard.

"That's enough for now." Will's tone relaxed. He leaned over and put a hand on Quinn's shoulder. "You should be out of here in a day or two. You'll be hobbling for a while, but you'll be fine."

"Thanks, Will."

"You cut it a bit close this time, Michael. Next time call in the damned cavalry."

As Will turned to leave, he stopped and pulled out his cell phone.

"Oh, there is one more thing. Almost forgot. The young lady."

"What young lady?"

"Miss Santorelli."

"Who?"

"Miss Sienna Santorelli?" Will was reading from his cell phone. "You remember, Marco's girlfriend. The one they tried to kidnap in Rome."

"Of course I remember." Quinn paused. "I—I never knew her last name. What about her?"

"She—well—she apparently wants to see you, my friend. To be exact, she wants to invite you to dinner when you are out of here. Says she wants to thank you." Will was staring at his phone, punching buttons with his thumbs. "I'm sending you her contact information now. Boy, is she a looker."

"Dinner? What the hell? How does she even know what happened to me?"

"At the Palazzo, she kept asking the police about you. That was relayed to the FBI, and then to us. We wanted to see if she knew anything, so we interviewed her. We confirmed that she knew absolutely nothing about any of this, and that her interest in you was purely social. So, I, ah, told her you were in a minor auto accident, and that you were going to be fine."

"And she believed you?"

"Sure. Although she kept calling back, asking about you. Remember, you've been out of it, unconscious and heavily sedated, for a few days."

"She kept asking about me?"

"Yes, Michael. Every single day."

CHAPTER 38

Laguna Beach, California

A RARE JUNE HEAT WAVE RIPPLED ACROSS THE SOUTHLAND, sending tourists and residents alike scrambling toward the seashore and clogging Pacific Coast Highway with traffic.

The spacious driveway of the Montage resort came up on Quinn's right. He swerved out of the chain of cars, onto the concrete curve, and pulled up under the portico of the hotel entrance.

When he climbed out of his car and stood up, the healing wounds down his back and leg screamed in protest, and his bandaged arms chafed against his shirt. The painkillers were wearing off. As he took his ticket from the valet, a welcoming sea breeze turned his thoughts to the evening ahead and the girl he was going to see.

Past the lobby and piano bar, a hallway wound along the back of the hotel. On his left were a series of small outdoor patios, with guests savoring the cooler temperatures and panoramic views of the sea.

His step slowed as he recognized the last patio. Cold memories of a previous night on that patio surfaced, of the man who had followed him there, of the steel knife glinting in the moonlight as it had gone for his throat. It wasn't long ago that Death had paid a visit to that pleasant little patio.

He turned his eyes away from the scene.

The pleasant aromas and soft chatter of the Loft wafted toward him, and he put a smile back on his face as he walked into the beach-bungalow charm of one of his favorite restaurants in the world.

Sienna waited for him at the table he would have picked— the table in the most secluded corner, next to the window with a view of the sea. It was, as before, those eyes. She stood to greet him, and as he grasped her offered hand he took in the rest of her.

The ash-blonde hair cascaded in graceful layers to her waist. She wore a turquoise jersey dress which clung to her athletic body. Spaghetti straps left her shoulders bare, as was, Quinn guessed, most of her upper back. The dress was cut low with a plunging neckline, her breasts jutting out against the thin fabric, their curves showing at the bottom of the V-shape. The turquoise fabric ended just above the knees, giving way to golden legs. The bare feet wore leather sandals.

She noticed Quinn wince slightly as he sat down.

"You are all right?" She looked him over. "Your associate at Global Art, he told me about your *accidente*. He did tell me you were in hospital, but kept telling me you were doing just fine. Going to be out in a day or so, he would tell me. He was so surprised when I kept asking about you. You did not mind?"

"Not at all. And yes, I'm fine. Just a couple of bruises. It was kind of you to inquire about me."

"It was the least I could do. Ah!" The green eyes flashed. "You save my life in Rome! I never got a chance to thank you.

Did I tell you I'm staying here at the Montage? I have a little room with a fireplace. And I've started my drawing again. In my room, I have an easel, paper, pencils, even my *pastelli*. So far, I ..."

Her voice trailed off, as if unsure what to say next.

"I-I guess we have some catching up to do, no?" she finished.

Quinn sensed the awkwardness of the moment and was determined to break the ice. Yes, in his career it was best to be a lone wolf. To never get involved.

Well, the hell with that. Life was too freaking short.

He wanted to get to know this girl. Something about her made him more ... *alive.*

He picked up the menus and handed her one.

"We certainly do, and let's start with nourishment. I would love to get better acquainted, Sienna, but let's do so over nectar and ambrosia. Coming off a diet of hospital food, the wine list and menu here look like gifts from the gods. Why don't we start with this Sauvignon Blanc and their local oysters?"

LATER

PALE GOLD MOONLIGHT CAST SHADOWS BEHIND THE COUPLE walking from the hotel walkway onto the deserted beach. White froth of black surf lapped at the sand.

A breeze tousled strands of Sienna's hair as she glanced over at Quinn. "I can ask you a personal question?"

"Absolutely." He smiled as he loosened his shirt collar. "But first we need to get our feet wet. Literally. I'm still hot and sweaty from the day, and I'm not about to walk on this beach in shoes."

Sienna removed her sandals, and then watched as he took off his shoes, socks, and sport coat. Making a blanket out of his folded coat, he laid their things on the sand and rolled up his pants above his knees and his shirtsleeves above his elbows. Brushing off Sienna's queries about his multiple bandages, he held her hand and led her down to the wet sand, where they stood and waited for the surf to roll in.

The three inches of frothy seawater were just enough to cover their feet, and Sienna giggled at the sensation. As they turned and walked along the wet sand, she moved closer, her body almost touching his. A faint scent of her body wash, the almonds and oranges he remembered from Rome, mixed with the sea air.

"I know so little about the world. You know a great deal, no? I would like you to show me."

"That might take a bit of time, Sienna."

"What is there that is more worth doing?" She hesitated. "Unless, of course, you are *obbligato*. Do you have a girlfriend?"

"No."

"A handsome man like you? You must have lots of girlfriends."

Quinn glanced at the golden girl strolling barefoot in the sand. "You've been through quite a lot. How does it feel to be free?"

She slowed her step as she thought. "Like a bow. Yes, that is it. An archer's bow. One where the bowstring, it has been pulled back, and back, and back."

They stopped to let the sea froth wash over their feet. She looked at Quinn. "And now let go."

Sienna gestured toward the far end of the curving sand. "I ran two miles on the beach here this morning, then went for a swim. It felt *fantastico*. I think I'll do it every morning I'm here.

Soon I'll know every part of this beach, from the little sand crabs to the sea gulls."

"Be sure to look out for the Pacific sea dragons then. They usually hang out behind that large group of rocks." Quinn pointed to a room-size jumble of black rock rising out from the sea.

"Sea dragons? You are joking, no?" The breeze tousled her hair and blew her dress against her body.

"Not at all. If you want to learn about the world, then we need to start with the local sights. The Pacific sea dragons are something to see. They're sort of a cross between a seal and a Komodo dragon. They're not found in the Mediterranean, only in the Pacific."

"That would explain why I haven't heard of them. Would they be out there now?" She took a cautious step out toward the sea.

"Possibly." Quinn stepped next to her and peered at the rock pile. "I believe they're nocturnal. We won't find out unless we get closer and have a look, will we? Come on, the water's receded. Let's go see."

He grabbed her by the hand, and they jogged out on the wet sand a dozen yards toward the sea. When they stopped and looked, the rock pile was more clearly defined.

"There! I see a sea dragon's tail moving, over there, behind that large rock." Quinn pointed.

"Where?" She brushed against him as she leaned over to see.

The touch of her skin was too much. His arm circled around and grabbed her firm tummy. Pulling her backside against him, his teeth bit into her inviting neck.

Sienna let out a sound that was a mix of a squeal and a giggle, then whirled around, placing her palm against his chest.

"You—"

The wave caught them both by surprise. The tide flowing

back in would have stopped below their knee level, but a small outcrop of rock near them turned a two-foot-high slice of onrushing water into a four-foot frothy wave, harmless, but just big enough to soak them both up to their shoulders.

Sienna shrieked as the cold sea water showered her body. Her shriek was cut short as Quinn pressed his mouth against hers and pulled her close. Her palm stayed against his chest, at first pushing back in protest, then relaxing in surrender.

The waters receded, and the kiss ended, but the two stood there in the sand, not wanting to unlock their embrace.

The thin jersey dress, soaked in sea water, clung to Sienna's body like a second skin. Through the cold, wet fabric Quinn could feel the warm curves where her waist met her backside. His hand slid up her body and caressed a tantalizing breast.

In the distance was the faint rushing sound of the tide coming back toward them.

"Well, we can't stay here forever. You'll catch cold. Did you mention your room has a fireplace?"

Sienna took a half step back and looked up at him with wide, innocent eyes. "There's an old Italian saying, Michael. To translate, rough I think you say, it is: 'When a woman gives her heart to a man, she is, she is handing him a loaded gun.'"

He brushed a drop of ocean spray off her cheek. She was shivering.

"Don't worry." He pressed her wet body against his.

"I never miss."

THE END

For more works by the author, please visit
www.kevinscottolson.com